D0935290

Date: 1/19/12

SCI FIC WELLS
Wells, H. G.
Star begotten :

PALM BEACH COUNTY
LIBRARY SYSTEM
3650 Summit Boulevard
West Palm Beach, FL 33406-4198

Star Begotten

THE

WESLEYAN

EARLY CLASSICS OF

SCIENCE FICTION

SERIES

General Editor

Arthur B. Evans

The Centenarian
  Honoré de Balzac

Cosmos Latinos:
An Anthology of Science Fiction
from Latin America and Spain
  Andrea L. Bell and Yolanda
  Molina-Gavilán, eds.

Caesar's Column:
A Story of the Twentieth Century
  Ignatius Donnelly

Subterranean Worlds:
A Critical Anthology
  Peter Fitting, ed.

Lumen
  Camille Flammarion

The Last Man
  Jean-Baptiste Cousin de
  Grainville

The Battle of the Sexes
in Science Fiction
  Justine Larbalestier

The Yellow Wave:
A Romance of the Asiatic
Invasion of Australia
  Kenneth Mackay

The Moon Pool
  A. Merritt

The Twentieth Century
  Albert Robida

The World as It Shall Be
  Emile Souvestre

Star Maker
  Olaf Stapledon

The Begum's Millions
  Jules Verne

Invasion of the Sea
  Jules Verne

The Mighty Orinoco
  Jules Verne

The Mysterious Island
  Jules Verne

H. G. Wells: Traversing Time
  W. Warren Wagar

Star Begotten: A Biological Fantasia
  H. G. Wells

Deluge
  Sydney Fowler Wright

ALSO BY JOHN HUNTINGTON

The H. G. Wells Reader, edited, 2003.

Ambition, Rank and Poetry in 1590s England, 2001.

Critical Essays on H. G. Wells, edited, 1991.

Rationalizing Genius:

   Ideological Strategies in the Classic American Science Fiction Short Story, 1989.

The Logic of Fantasy: H. G. Wells and Science Fiction, 1982.

EDITED BY JOHN HUNTINGTON

Star Begotten

A Biological Fantasia

by H. G. Wells

WESLEYAN UNIVERSITY PRESS   Middletown, Connecticut

Published by

Wesleyan University Press,

Middletown, CT 06459

www.wesleyan.edu/wespress

Introduction and scholarly materials

copyright © 2006 by John Huntington.

Copyright by The Literary Executors of

the Estate of H G Wells.

All rights reserved

Printed in the United States of America

Title page art © PhotoDisc

Cataloging-in-Publication Data is available

from the Library of Congress

ISBN 0-8195-6729-9 Cloth

ISBN 0-8195-6730-2 Paper

5   4   3   2   1

Contents

Acknowledgments

Wells studies is populated by a host of deeply informed, intelligent, and helpful scholars, and an edition such as this owes a great debt to the whole field of scholarship. The two readers for Wesleyan University Press have read carefully and made useful criticisms and suggestions. Their attention to detail assures me that the edition is finally free of gross blunders. Arthur Evans, the general editor of the Wesleyan Early Classics of Science Fiction Series, first urged me to pursue the project of producing an edition of *Star Begotten*. At a later stage when I had become stymied by the mystery of permissions, Suzanna Tamminen at the press gave the project a boost by putting me in touch with A. P. Watt, Ltd., the agent for the Wells estate. My wife, Virginia Wright Wexman, as always, read, advised, and encouraged throughout. Without her there would be nothing.

Introduction

In 1937, when he was seventy years old, H. G. Wells published *Star Begotten*, the second of a series of four short novels that would appear within two years.[1] The cluster of novels follows closely on the film *Things to Come*, one of Wells's many attempts to invent an imagery and construct a narrative sufficient to address both the long range future of humankind—on which he had been meditating since as early as *The Time Machine*—and the much more immediate future of European civilization in the late 1930s, challenged by fascism and threatened by war.[2]

Star Begotten is another of these attempts. It recounts the life of the idea that Martians are using cosmic rays to alter human chromosomes and thus to take over the Earth. It describes how Joseph Davis, an author of popular histories, gets obsessed with the idea, worries about the birth of his child, and finally reconciles himself to the possibility that the mutation has already occurred and that he himself may be a Martian. Much of the novel involves discussions among three men —Davis, Professor Ernst Keppel, and Dr. Holdman Stedding—about whether such an invasion is plausible and what it might mean. Midway through the story, popularizers and the press get hold of the idea and manipulate it, but the fad soon recedes. It is a very simple story; compared to any of the early scientific romances or even to *Things to Come*, it is hardly a narrative at all.

Most contemporary reviewers, even favorable ones, tended to read *Star Begotten* as belonging to the familiar utopian, scientific romance genre long associated with Wells. Typical is Ralph Thompson in the *New York Times*: "One might think that after forty years of scientific romancing H. G. Wells would be sick and tired of Other Worlds. But he isn't; he can't be. His fantastic yarns about the solar system are part of what must be called, for lack of a better term, his faith. The most recent is also one of the best: 'Star-Begotten.'"[3] A few reviewers, however, sensed something more than a "fantastic yarn" in *Star Begotten*. One Canadian reviewer saw clearly that Wells does not give us "another imaginative picture." "Perhaps," she opined, "he has tired of writing imaginative pictures for those who will not understand his meaning."[4] She echoes here Wells himself; in his preface to *The Scientific Romances* (1933), he had made exactly such a complaint: "Work of this sort gets so stupidly reviewed nowadays that it has little chance of being properly read. . . . It becomes a bore doing imaginative books that do not touch imaginations, and at length one stops even planning them."[5] Wells's dilemma, here in the endgame of his career, is that the very strength of his reputation as the father of the scientific romance—by this time being called sometimes "scientifiction" and sometimes "science fiction" in the United States—has caused expectations to become so formulaic that the ideas at work in the fictions no longer stimulate real thought.[6] One suspects that Ms. Grube is right, that *Star Begotten* is something other than a scientific romance.

No one would say that *Star Begotten* is "obscure," but its form is eccentric and its meaning is remarkably difficult to pin down. Like another Martian invasion which was produced just a year later—the radio broadcast of Orson Welles—the novel gains force and importance from the feeling of panic in the air in 1937. V. S. Pritchett, always a Wells enthusiast, saw it tapping into our own fears and hopes. The idea of the Martian mutation, Pritchett declared in one of his reviews, is "allegorically right," and it "catches us on the full wave of our wish."[7] Such a defense, suggesting that the story is "allegorical" and attributing its force not to the story but to "the full wave of our wish," speaks to the urgency of the issues behind *Star Begotten*, but it tells us little about the way the novel actually works. Perceptive reviewers sensed that something was up in this novel, that the genre of the scientific romance was being manipulated, but they didn't—or couldn't—say what exactly was happening.

In part confusion arises because Wells is often thought of as writing clear, simple, and, in his later years, optimistic fictions. Many readers would agree with Virginia Woolf's notorious criticism of him in her 1924 essay on the Edwardian novelists, which treats him as a reductive utopianist. In her thought experiment about "Mrs. Brown"—

how would different Edwardian novelists depict a shabby woman on a train?—Woolf envisions Wells as writing this way:

> Mr. Wells would instantly project upon the window-pane a vision of a better, breezier, jollier, happier, more adventurous and gallant world, where these musty railway carriages and fusty old women do not exist; where miraculous barges bring tropical fruit to Camberwell by eight o'clock in the morning; where there are public nurseries, fountains, and libraries, dining-rooms, drawing-rooms, and marriages; where every citizen is generous and candid, manly and magnificent, and rather like Mr. Wells himself. But nobody is in the least like Mrs. Brown. There are no Mrs. Browns in Utopia. Indeed I do not think that Mr. Wells, in his passion to make her what she ought to be, would waste a thought upon her as she is.[8]

This strikes home, and one can even find elements—"where every citizen is generous and candid, manly and magnificent"—that seem to anticipate moments in *Star Begotten* when Professor Kepple imagines the Martianized future. Once one has this idea of Wells, it is difficult to grant him artistic subtlety.

Wells himself, in his character of utopian polemicist, contributes to this simple impression by depicting himself as an uncomplicated thinker. He had been educated as a biologist. What he would later call "the most educational year of my life" was spent under the tutelage of the great colleague and defender of Darwin, T. H. Huxley. Like many people trained in science, he found himself uninterested in "art," in the style of argument that spends time admiring its own complexities. As he described himself in *The Fate of Man*, written right after *Star Begotten*, he is direct, impatient with ambiguity, not afraid to state the bare facts:

> The peculiar strength and the peculiar weakness of my mind are one and the same quality. Put favorably, mine is a very direct mind; put unfavorably, it is unsubtle. I am impatient of complicating details and conventional misstatements because I am afraid of them. The reader will find this book [*The Fate of Man*] ego-centered, for so

we all began, and also insistent, I *hammer* at my main ideas, and this is an offense to delicate-minded people. If a door is not open I say it is shut, and I am impatient with the suggestion of worldly wisdom that it may be possible to wangle a way round. Yet there may be a way round if you do not lose yourself getting there.[9] You have been warned that I shall not be with you in any such uncertain enterprise. I work not simply for knowledge but for a stark clarity of thought about it. It seems to me a fair challenge to demand a lucid statement of the vision of the universe to which this directness of inquiry and assemblage have brought me.[10]

From such a utopian social scientist trying to change the world one would expect an unambiguous vision of "stark clarity."

Wells the novelist, however, sees things in a more dramatic and conflicted form. In his preface to *Babes in the Darkling Wood* (1940), he defends once more his conception of the novel of "ideas."[11] The novelist, unlike the political thinker, advocates living "dialogue" in place of a "lucid statement of the vision of the universe." "As soon as you tear a brain away from its blood and membranes: it dies. Abstract philosophy is the deadest of stuff; one disintegrating *hortus siccus* follows another; I am astounded at the implacable scholarly industry of those who still write Textbooks of Philosophy."[12] The arguments and the characters in the fiction of ideas need to be convincing and recognizable, though their dialogue is not a realistic transcription of the way people talk but a rendering of "what they imagined they were saying, and what indeed they meant."[13] The point of such dialogue is not to preach, but to give shape to ideas and make them and their struggle real. In the preface to *Babes in the Darkling Wood*, Wells insists that "these talkers" were not "self-projections," as some readers claimed. "These obtrusive individuals were not saying things I thought, but, what is a very different thing, things I wanted to put into shape by having them said."[14] Wells is trying to articulate a situation and an argument in its dialogic dynamic, and his interest is, finally, more ironic than is often realized. He is ironic, not to satirize or to draw laughs, but as a way of trying to see more than any of the individual speakers in the dialogue can master—of seeing the ideas as they stand in competition with others, often their contraries.

The works that such a dialogic novelist creates are not clear and direct. Unlike doors—"If a door is not open I say it is shut"—human feelings and social acts are not binary, not just open or closed, and the rendering of such positions is going to require something more than straightforward statement or description. Despite his protestations of "directness," Wells was too mischievous and too savvy about the ways of the world and of the psyche just to recite a simple story. From the very beginning, with the time traveler who was too clever to be trusted or believed,[15] Wells has questioned the innocent and naive reading of stories. *Star Begotten* is important because it shows Wells, late in his career and at a historical moment when everyone is talking crisis, exploring the possible self-deceptions that motivate the utopian idea and the ambiguities inherent in strong positions.[16] While at some level the most uncomplicated of tales, it is perhaps at the same time the most thoroughly and teasingly ambiguous of all Wells's works.

Ambiguity will out. Even readers committed to unambiguous readings tend to find that as they go deeper into *Star Begotten* they are led into difficulties. For instance, Olaf Stapledon's review of the novel draws attention to an inconsistency. As the author of three recent novels about the extrahuman possibilities for human growth and a nonfiction utopian work,[17] Stapledon seems to want a novel that will pose the Martian idea without skepticism.[18] But, curiously, at the end of his review, his own skepticism is roused: because he accepts as true Joseph Davis's final revelation of his own Martian nature, Stapledon finds he must object that there are no signs earlier of his superior Martian mentality. Would a true Martian have pursued the kind of compromised career that Davis has up to this point? Davis, Stapledon suggests, is not shown as exceptional; he "was disturbed by a spark, but this is true of most men."[19] This is eminently reasonable logic, and it can be extended backward to call not only Davis but the whole fantasy of the Martian transformation into question. Put another way, Stapledon's own eagerness to hear about superhuman possibilities has led him to find a flaw when he may actually have identified a central ambiguity of the novel.

In a review appearing in *Nature*, J. B. S. Haldane sees Wells turning on his own utopian proposals of the past and posing a biological solution to the world's problems.[20] Appropriately, given the interests of the journal for which he is writing, Haldane sketches some of the scientific impossibilities on which the novel is based. He suspects that Wells himself is skeptical of the book's science, that it offers "a panacea which he [i.e. Wells] knows to be fantastic." Finally, Haldane argues, because the evolutionary timescale is so long and the crisis is so immediate, the Martian mutation can't work. Haldane, a Marxist, makes a point at the beginning about Wells's anticommunism and even finds a kind of unconscious pun in the novel: for *Martian* read *Marxian*. He concludes: "If this book encourages a single reader to think, even for one moment, that any natural or supernatural process will take the place of human effort and human thought, then it is a bad book." Thus Haldane argues against fantasies of biological redemption. The revolution will come not from bigger brains but from "human effort and human thought."[21] But Haldane also senses a different way of reading Wells's novel: "But if it is read as a record of conversations between rather worried intellectuals, it is not only an excellent piece of writing, but also a valuable historical document." The specific options Haldane allows—believe in outside help or see the novel as a vaguely admirable "piece of writing"—are left hanging. But behind this set of interpretive alternatives lurks a deeper insight into the very doubleness of the novel itself. As in the case of Stapledon, whose spiritual expectation has blinded him to the implications of his analysis, Haldane's insight into the novel's doubleness is an accurate reading that has been distorted by the stern commands of his own political perspective.

If Haldane and Stapledon read the ideas in *Star Begotten* seriously, so did Wells. Because his training with T. H. Huxley had taught him a rigorous Darwinism, Wells had from the beginning made it a rule that he would rebuke attempts to misuse the theory of evolution. Whatever fantasies about possibilities the early scientific romances may have indulged in, they were correct on their evolutionary theory. Five years before publishing *Star Begotten*, Wells, in collaboration with his son, G. P.

Wells, and Julian Huxley, had completed the massive work *The Science of Life*, a lengthy summary of the state of biology at the time that was uncompromising in its dismissal of distortions of evolutionary theory. At one point *The Science of Life* takes George Bernard Shaw and Henri Bergson to task for turning the basic principles of natural selection into a positive, teleological drive that easily "may relapse from Evolution to the older conception of Transformation."[22] Natural selection, the text insists, is not purposeful, and it is not a matter of the species simply mutating into a "higher" being. The important point, which such mystical ideas of purpose ignore, is that the theory of natural selection is a process not of directed creation but of selective culling by the forces of environment: "The crises of Evolution when they occur are not crises of variation but of selection and elimination; *not strange births, but selective massacres*."[23]

Even in a discussion of how X-rays stimulate mutation—the idea at the center of *Star Begotten*—*The Science of Life* insists that "mutation seems in general to be a perfectly random process. There is no evidence of adaptive striving or set purpose in the way new varieties turn up. The race varies in all directions at random, in a manner as casual and apparently purposeless as the desultory X-ray bombardment that may be the variations' cause. Out of these random purposeless gropings of the race Evolution builds."[24] The authors even apologize for repeating the point: "We lay this much stress on this fact that selection *is* selection and not production, not because we lack any respect for our readers' intelligence, but because there exists a voluminous foolish literature of controversy in which Darwin is alleged to have taught that natural Selection, in Heaven knows what inconceivable way, *produced* variations."[25] According to the usual reading, *Star Begotten* would seem to belong to that "voluminous foolish literature" that sees a directed variation as scientifically plausible. But, as we shall see, the novel in fact takes considerable pains to warn us against this reading.

Wells's Darwinism did not make him a pessimist; his hopes for a better future, however, were based on intensive and enlightened education rather than on biological evolution. At the very close of the section on evolution, *The Science of Life* argues that any purpose that can be found in human development is created by conscious humanity itself, not nature, and proceeds by education, not by mutation. Confusion arises because the two processes, evolution and education, can share a common vocabulary of development and growth.

> Now that consciousness has awakened in life, it has at last become possible to hope for a speedier and less wasteful method of evolution, a method based on foresight and deliberate planning instead of the old slow method of blind struggle and blind selection. At present that is no more than a hope. But human knowledge and power have grown very marvelously during the last few hundred years. The multitude of our race living to-day still does not know more than a minute fraction of what is known to man, nor dream yet of the things he may presently do.[26]

This is an ambiguous passage: could "Martianizing" be implied in the phrase "Human knowledge and power have grown"? In another work of this period, *Science and the World Mind*, we find Wells himself arguing that the world has radically changed and "like any other species of animal, [man] has to adapt himself to these changes in his conditions, or perish as a species. He may be extinguished altogether, or he may undergo modification into a new species. There is no question of his remaining as he is. The question is whether he can adapt himself with sufficient rapidity to become either a progressive super-*Homo*, an ascendant species, or one of a series of degenerating sub-human species, or whether he will fail altogether to adapt himself, and end altogether."[27] In this context a phrase like "he can adapt himself" might sound like eugenicist biology, but a page later it turns out that the "adaptation" Wells seems to be envisioning is a social one. "Every generation of *Homo sapiens* can learn the mental adaptation that has been imposed by altered conditions upon its predecessor."[28] If in the natural course of evolution, as a nameless voice in *Star Begotten* reminds us, "Transmission of acquired characteristics [is] strictly forbidden" (61) here in the social world, thanks to education and its replacing natural selection, it is exactly this Lamarkian process, the passing on of acquired characteristics, that prevails.[29]

It is education that Wells repeatedly returns to as the hope for humankind in the terrible time just before World War II, not the genetically engineered superman. In his collection *World Brain*, published the year after *Star Begotten*, Wells begins by insisting that "In the human being there is an unprecedented extension of educability; not only is learning developed to relatively immense proportions, but it is further supplemented by curiosity, precept and tradition. In such a slow-breeding creature as man educational adaptation is beyond all comparison a swifter process than genetic adaptation."[30] In a lecture he gave in September 1937, Wells attacked traditional education for wasting the small amount of time we are granted to teach young humans. "We have no time to waste, if our schools are not to go on delivering, year by year, fresh hordes of fundamentally ignorant, unbalanced, uncritical minds, at once suspicious and credulous, weakly gregarious, easily baffled and easily misled, into the monstrous responsibilities and dangers of this present world. Mere cannon-fodder and stuff for massacres and stampedes."[31] I draw attention to this powerful and urgent aspect of Wells's argument in 1937 because it operates even when *Star Begotten* seems to move in other directions. We have the minds, he argues; we need to set up a worldwide structure of education and cooperation to bring out the potentials of those minds.

Star Begotten is an uncomplicated tale with a single scientific idea at its center that turns out to be ambiguous at every level. Like Henry James's *The Turn of the Screw* half a century earlier, the novel uses ambiguity to probe the rationality of hysteria. I raise the specter of James at this point because in part Wells's late novel, by adapting a Jamesian technique, does one further turn in the long battle over the novel that was most explicitly enunciated in their conflict in the second decade of the twentieth century. Here in the fourth decade of the century Wells questions narrative simplicity. As a sort of self-consuming artifact, *Star Begotten* is always asking us to doubt the validity of the reasoning its characters bring to the problem of the world crisis. The novel poses SF as an essentially ironic mode that, while seeming to look away from current events, comments on them. The fantasy concludes by criticizing itself as fantasy.

Such ambiguity is not characteristic of the traditional scientific romance. While it certainly puts in play an idea that befits a scientific romance, *Star Begotten* is curiously reluctant to make the essential imaginative move that identifies this form.[32] The great early works, such as *The Time Machine*, *The Invisible Man*, or that first novel about the Martians, *The War of the Worlds*, all take considerable pains to imagine how the impossible might happen, what it would look like, sound like, feel like, and how it would influence the world. In the genre-establishing early works, Wells memorably pictured the time machine itself and the experience of time travel, the man who is invisible, the Martians and their machines. The paradigm, as exemplified by *The Time Machine*, is to pose an impossibility, challenge it theoretically for a moment, and then "show" it as a fact. After this moment of skepticism the impossibility goes unquestioned: time travel, human invisibility, Martian invaders, Cavorite, Boom-food, and all the other lovely, impossible ideas are treated as undeniably real. *Star Begotten*, instead of using action and detail to create a new world, confines itself just to talk. This novel never depicts a Martian. It even gives us reasons to doubt the central scientific idea that drives the story.

The novel's opening lines put us in an ambiguous situation. "This is the story of an idea and how it played about in the minds of a number of intelligent people" (37). This line could mean that there is an idea behind this story (i.e., this is a story about a Martian invasion and how people thought about it). Or we might just as well read it as a story about how an idea takes hold (i.e., it is a story about how the *idea* of such an invasion lives and dies). The ambiguity is not clarified in the next line: "Whether there was any reality behind this idea it is not the business of the storyteller to say." This could mean simply that this is a story, not an actual warning about such an invasion (who knows what the actual Martians are planning!), but it could just as well mean that even *in the fiction of the story* it unclear whether or not there is a real Martian invasion. "The reader must judge for himself": that is, either the reader can simply choose which way to read it, or it is the purpose of the novel to make the reader examine this "reality" closely and come to an interpretation.

The relatively abstract questions that Wells himself has raised in the opening lines of the novel about how we are to determine what is real loom ever larger in the absence of confirming "fact" in the narrative. The remarkable dynamic of the novel is that on the basis of empty supposition with only some very random anecdotal evidence, the idea of the Martian invasion becomes convincing to some of the characters. These men, who perhaps ought to know better, find themselves first subscribing to the idea of mutation and then later imagining a vague utopian possibility which may finally have no more reality than a castle in air. Or, put somewhat differently, if the art of the scientific romance consists of creating an illusion by "precision in the unessential and vagueness in the essential,"[33] *Star Begotten* reverses things. It repeatedly withholds the details that might make the much-discussed idea "work." The novel, subtitled *A Fantasia*, never does what scientific romances do: it never *shows* the fantastic.

Wells could easily have made the planned evolution of humanity by mutation caused by cosmic rays from Mars a plausible idea. He had before him the example of Stapledon's *Odd John* (1935). Within a few years the idea of such mutation would be a commonplace—witness Arthur C. Clarke's depiction of a "new" mentality showing up in children in *Childhood's End*. Wells not only refuses to make the idea happen, he explicitly goes out of his way to debunk the idea every time it is raised. Even the most positive discussions of the possibility are ambiguous stand-offs. The very cornerstone of the theory is left unconfirmed: when Foxfield, the biologist who started the discussion, asserts that cosmic rays cause mutations, an older scientist declares, "You'll find no physicist to encourage you [in this theory]." After Foxfield discounts the importance of positive evidence and counters the older man with, "Or contradict me," the older scientist agrees and concludes, "It's a case of not proven" (60). Such might be the epigraph of the novel itself.

Even the most unchallenged versions of the theory emphasize the playfulness of the line of thought. In an elegantly and distractingly self-referential passage, Wells develops the seeds of the theory out of a piece of "impossible" fiction. Suppose the rays come from Mars, a man exclaims:

"Mars, the planet which is being frozen out, exhausted, done for. Some of you may have read a book called *The War of the Worlds*—I forget who wrote it—Jules Verne, Conan Doyle, one of those fellows. But it told how the Martians invaded the world, wanted to colonize it and exterminate mankind. Hopeless attempt! They couldn't stand the different atmospheric pressure, they couldn't stand the difference in gravitation; bacteria finished them up. Hopeless from the start. The only impossible thing in the story was to imagine that the Martians would be fools enough to try anything of the sort. But—. . . [s]uppose they say up there: 'Let's start varying and modifying life on the earth. Let's change it. Let's get at the human character and the human brain and make it Martian-minded. Let's stop having children on this rusty little old planet of ours, and let's change men until they become in effect *our* children. Let's get spiritual children there.' D'you see? Martian minds in seasoned terrestrial bodies. . . . And presently. . . . when they have got the world Martianized—" (62)

Wells seems to be taking some pleasure in the radically hypothetical ("suppose they say . . .") nature of an idea generated not out of any scientific knowledge but out of a fantasy about Martian psychology. At this point, in a devastating comment on the unscientific basis of this line of thought, the older scientist who had earlier explained basic physics, after insisting that the cosmic rays do not all come from the direction of Mars, walks out in disgust.

Once that skeptic is out of the room, however, the fantasy builds: "And when they have got the world Martianized, when they've started a race here with minds like their own and yet with bodies fit for earth, when they have practically interbred with us and ousted our strain, *then* they'll begin to send along their treasures, their apparatus—*grafting* their life on ours. Making men into their heirs and their continuation" (63). The language here is comically evasive. How is it possible to get from genetic manipulation to "practically interbred"? Somehow sending "along their treasures, their apparatus" becomes "grafting." In a line that both keeps the idea afloat and dismisses it, Foxcroft acknowledges that "the jokes of today may become the facts of tomorrow" (63).

This can be read to say that what is here imagined might come to pass, but it also identifies the discussion as a "joke." The implausibility of the joke is emphasized when he warns that "Nine hundred and Ninety-nine per cent [sic]"[34] of natural mutations are unfavorable, "with no survival value at all" (64). With that, the discussion breaks off, but despite the ridicule an essential linkage of ideas—one can't call it a theory—has been set in motion.

Wells goes to considerable lengths to make us aware of the logical problems involved in accepting the theory of Martian mutations. If we were to see "empirical" evidence, that would circumvent the logical issue, but all we see is the desire that the barely "possible" become probable. Mr. Davis raises the possibility of Martian experiments on human genes, and when Dr. Holdman Stedding asks how, Davis replies:

> "You have heard of cosmic rays, Doctor?"
>
> The doctor took it in with some deliberation. "It is a *quite* fantastic idea," he said after a pause.
>
> "But neither impossible nor incredible."
>
> "Some things one puts outside the range of practical possibility."
>
> "And some things refuse to be put outside the range of practical possibility."
>
> "But you don't mean to tell me you believe—?"
>
> "No. But I face a possibility with an open mind."
>
> "Which is?"
>
> "That these Martians—?"
>
> "But we don't know there *are* any Martians!"
>
> "We don't know that there aren't."
>
> "No."
>
> "Quite possibly these rays do not come from Mars—more probably than not. But—let us call the senders—"
>
> "*Senders?*"
>
> "Well, whatever originates them. Let us call them Martians—just to avoid inventing a new name—" (69)

Thus, while never claiming to "believe," conceding that the rays probably do not come from Mars,[35] insisting on the reality of the merely "possible," Mr. Davis and the doctor end up in a discussion of the intentions of nonexistent Martians and their fantastic technology of "cosmic rays." It is hard to imagine Wells rendering this absurd discussion without some pleasure in its illogicality.

Davis is relentless in his claim to be disinterested while at the same time insisting that the slightest possibility must be taken seriously. In response to Dr. Holdman Steddings's exclamation, "But you don't *believe*—?" Mr. Davis can quickly (and disingenuously) say "Not a bit of it, Oh, no! I didn't come here to be certified. I am advancing a certain hypothesis" (70). Moments later he escalates the stakes: "If there is one chance in a million of this suspicion being true, then it demands attention" (71). This is a version of Pascal's wager.[36] As William Empson neatly argues, a person who accepts such logic is "the slave of any person professing any doctrine, who has the impudence to tell him a sufficiently extravagant lie."[37] In the next couple of chapters this same kind of logic leads to the conclusion that Martians probably exist, that they are bigger than we are (because of the lighter gravity on Mars), that they therefore have larger brains, that therefore they are smarter than we are, and that therefore they are benign.[38] On a basis of this entirely hypothetical argument we arrive at the conclusion that "The odds are they are not so much invading us as acting as a sort of interplanetary tutor" (81).

The irony is that Joseph Davis has always lived in such a logically slippery world. Wells's objections to modern education cited above might have been formulated with Davis in mind. Throughout the first chapter Wells depicts the ironies of Joseph Davis's orthodox adolescent development and draws our attention to the social compromises involved in arriving at understanding. When Davis's childish trust in the biblical stories comes into conflict with his developing sense of reality, the techniques by which the scientific answers are dismissed are neatly rendered in the aesthetic language of the argument. "He acquired a great contempt for 'mere size' and that kept astronomy in its place" (40). It is by a similarly aesthetic judgment that Mr. Davis dismisses all the questions the universe raises about the unique salvation of a small group of people on Earth. Mr. Davis "realized that he had been much *too crude* in feeling uncomfortable about that early Bible narrative and the scheme of salvation and all the rest of it. As a matter-of-fact statement it was *not perhaps in the coarser sense true*, but that was because of the infirmities of language and the peculiar low state of Eastern Levantine intelligence and Eastern Levantine moral ideas when the hour to 'reveal' religion had struck" (41, emphases added). *Crude* and *coarse* are hardly logical terms. To ask that something stand up to the criticism of fact—that is, to hold up a scientific standard—is to be vulgar. In the following passage, it is the touches of contempt ("really did not matter," "rationalist stuff," "contemptibly crude") and admiration ("great ritual of ceremonial," "co-ordinating fabric of . . . social life") that make the argument.

> It was being conveyed to him that it really did not matter what foundations of myth or fantasy the existing system of Western civilization was built upon; the fact that mattered was that it was built upon that foundation and that a great ritual of ceremonial and observance, which might be logically unmeaning, and an elaborate code of morality, which might ultimately prove to be arbitrary, nevertheless constituted the co-ordinating fabric of current social life and that social life could not now go on without them. So that all this freethinker and rationalist stuff became irrelevant and indeed contemptibly crude. (41)

To challenge the thing that *is* would be to undermine the system that *works*: "He was left face to face with history and society. Christianity and its churches, the monarchy and political institutions, the social hierarchy, seemed to be regarding him blandly. It is no good inquiring into our credentials now, they seemed to say. Here we are. We work. (They seemed to be working then.) And what other reality is there?" (42).

Davis is himself a sort of anti-Wells: where Wells focused on science, Davis has shunned science in school. Where Wells had from the start set himself up to challenge the complacencies of the age, Davis wrote "heartening and stalwart books" that "gird[ed] remorselessly at dissidence and doubt" (43). Where Wells's *Outline of History* had been written to demystify human history, Davis has set himself the project of writing a "deliberately romanticized history of mankind" (43) with the tentative title *Grand Parade of Humanity*. "He had made himself a champion of that ancient and venerable normal life of humanity, unaltered through the ages—except now and then through the providential punishment of some transitory heresy—the simple, old, beautiful story of childhood, learning, love, industry, parentage, honour, and the easy passage to a venerable old age and a brightly hopeful death" (86). This is precisely the kind of history Wells himself denounces:

> So far as my convictions go I think that the less young children have either in or out of school of what has hitherto figured as *history*, the better. I do not see either the charm or the educational benefit of making an important subject of and throwing a sort of halo of prestige and glory about the criminal history of royalty. . . . I suggest that the sooner we get all that unpleasant stuff out of schools . . . the nearer our world will be to a sane outlook upon life.[39]

In his sentimental nationalism, the early Joseph Davis recalls other author figures in late Wells who tend to show up as reactionary and deluded traditionalists. Theodore Bulpington, the main character in *The Bulpington of Blup*, writes the same kind of uplifting national histories as Davis does. Bulpington, however, ends up an explicit fascist. Rowland Palace in *Brynhild* is a somewhat less obviously politically reactionary, but he too takes pride in empty uplift. He disappears from the novel to spend his time in carefully engineered self-promotion. Davis represents the world of literary complacency that Wells has fought all his life.[40]

The parochial chauvinism of such a posture generates a structurally necessary xenophobia. Though the narrator concedes that "here there seems to have been some gap in his logical process" (86), "These Martians presented themselves to [Davis] as the blackest of threats to all those convictions that make life worth living upon earth. Indisputably they must be *inhuman*, whatever else they are. That went without saying. To be inhuman implied to him, as to most of us, malignant cruelty" (87). In a remarkable self-reflective moment Wells uses this occasion to meditate on how for Davis the more mentally superior the Martians are, the worse they must be. "It was an intolerable thought for him that there should appear any class of creatures on earth, intellectually above his own, unless they were profoundly inferior to him morally, and so repulsive and ugly as practically to reverse the handicap against him" (87). With such motivations, Davis imagines Martians very like those that invade England in Wells's own *The War of the Worlds.*

Davis lives a difficult psychic life in this novel, and the nagging sense that he is never thinking clearly but is always working around unacknowledged personal difficulties undercuts even his most rational-seeming ideas. Dr. Holdman Stedding suspects that "mentally he was not too safely balanced" (75), and at one time cites Davis "as an example of the extreme intellectual elaboration that may appear in a case of delusional insanity" (95). Early in the novel Davis has begun to question the nationalist orthodoxies he has based his career on, and "this peculiar feeling—mental duplicity shall we call it?—this doubt of himself" (46) links up with a moment of strange anxiety about his wife to produce the crisis which leads him to fix on the Martian idea. Mary, his wife, herself seems to be going through a reconsideration of her life: she has, as she puts it, "done" music, and, referring to their conventional life together, she bluntly tells Davis, "I don't know whether I care for very much more of this sort of thing unless I am going to have a child." Davis is sensitive to the power of her simple language to call into question the basis of his whole world. "*This sort of thing!* Roses, raptures, whispers, dusk, moonlight, nightingales, all the love poetry that ever was—*this sort of thing!*" (48). The dismissive phrase cannot be answered, so it must be repressed. By agreeing to have a child, "he buried 'this sort of thing' as deeply as he could under high-piled flower-beds of philoprogenitive sentiments; he tried his utmost to forget her strangely inhuman phrase" (48).

With considerable subtlety Wells links this unexpressed anxiety intrinsic in Davis's relation with his wife to his concern with the Martian idea. In a wonderfully layered moment, we are told that if the gynecologist, Dr. Holdman Stedding, had asked if Davis were concerned about an influence of the Martian rays on his pregnant wife, Davis "would have answered at once with almost perfect honesty that these Martian speculations of his had absolutely nothing to do with her. But he would not have answered the question calmly; he would have had a touch of defensive indignation in his voice. And it was not a question he could have asked himself. It was a question he could not have asked himself; there was some barrier against that" (88). In that "almost," in the defensiveness, in even the very subtle shift of the negative from the question ("not a question he could have asked") to the psychic action ("a question he could not have asked"), we hear fine distinctions of repression at work (could he not have thought of it, or would he have had the thought but never have allowed himself to acknowledge it?). Later, even after his son is born healthy, Davis is never quite straight and even contradicts himself to deny how intensely he has cathected with the Martian idea. After he has insisted on the Martian theory, he can in the next chapter claim, "I never said they were Martians," and then immediately turn around and say "why trouble about the name? Let us stick to Martians" (108). He is trapped in an obsession that he cannot quite justify; it peeks out in devious ways.

Another side of Davis, however, begins to recognize other possibilities. On a visit to a school to give a lecture, he discovers a schoolboy who asks "what is spiritual?" (93). In the interesting discussion with the headmaster about the case, we hear orthodoxy defended by the latter in terms that one expects Davis to acknowledge: "But you see, Mr. Davis, the fundamental things of life cannot be defined" (93). When he is safely outside, however, Davis rejects the headmaster's argument. It is the very dissatisfaction with the accepted and the unquestioned that comes to mark the Martian for Davis. "They don't see life as we see it. They can't think of it in our way. And they make us begin to doubt that we see it ourselves as we have always imagined we did" (94). Unlike the other pompous establishment authors Wells was depicting, Davis becomes capable of reflecting on how downright misleading his seemingly harmless narratives have been and acknowledging the vain uselessness of his supposedly heroic art. Late in the novel, having worked long and hard on his history, he burns the manuscript.

Given the subterranean psychological reading of Davis's interest in the Martian idea, the final turn of the novel must open the possibility that what Stapledon saw as a flaw in the novel's logic is in fact an intended meaning: Davis's epiphanic insight that he himself is Martian is not the novel's conclusion about reality but the final stage of his delusion. When he is first introduced, we hear that he does not like his name; *Joseph* lacks "virility." The joke about the savior's parents is set up here. At the heart of Davis's anxiety is a doubt about his fatherhood. He has a long discussion with Dr. Holdman Stedding in which bit by bit he reveals the Martian fantasy until he finally arrives at the position, "that presently our very children may not prove to be our own" (71), a line the doctor recalls and repeats. When Dr. Holdman Stedding unintentionally hints at this biblical paradigm after the child is born—"There's not a painted Madonna in all the world with a lovelier bambino than hers"—Davis is made uneasy and "was minded to go out and not to see Mary for a time" (89). Like the biblical Joseph, he feels like an extraneous person in the nativity. Finally, when Mary herself—"Would the jest offend him?" (140)—identifies him as a Martian, it is this insecurity that causes him to accept the idea instantly and with relief. "He too was star-born! He too was one of these invaders and strangers and innovators to our fantastic planet, who were crowding into life and making it over anew! Throwing the torn scraps into a basket and beginning again in the nursery. Fantastic how long it had taken him to realize this!" (140). The alien has become the human; all enlightened people are Martians. This is both a revelation and a trivialization of the fantasy. When Davis includes his wife among the star begotten, "She nodded agreement. If he wished it, so be it" (140). It is an act of loving charity for her to go along with Davis's fantasy, just as earlier in the novel she has volunteered to accompany him to a concert despite her headache and her lack of interest in music. Perhaps the whole novel is a not very serious delusion.

Delusion in *Star Begotten* is serious, very serious, just not in the way sometimes supposed. In between the early inklings of Martian influence and the later imaginings of the "sane" world to come, the novel indulges in a pair of highly satiric explorations of the way the idea of the Martian mutation works when it becomes public. Here we see the forces working against education and sanity. In the hands of men like Harold Rigamey and Lord Thunderclap, education will again be reduced to producing the "Mere cannon-fodder and stuff for massacres and stampedes" that Wells complained of elsewhere.

Rigamey is a parody of Wells himself, a popularizer of science, but an irresponsible one who, to create an illusion, "invoked almost every known authority upon extra-terrestrial radiations, produced in a skillfully clipped form some rare unguarded statements by eminent professors, promoted one or two rash speculations by obscure people in remote parts of the earth to a distinguished scientific standing, and invented a few anonymous scientists of his own" (97). He gives the aura of scientific authority to irresponsible rumor and puts in play such phrases as "The Martian genes" and "The Martian Type": "And so [he] told the whole story as we have already seen it unfolding in the mind of Mr. Joseph Davis, but with a richness of confirmatory detail altogether beyond our modest record of actualities" (98). The joke here, of course, is that compared to Rigamey, Wells, the author of this "Biological Fantasia," is the responsible one.

Lord Thunderclap is both more comic and more dangerous. A press-lord of enormous power, he is revealed as paranoid and as the puppet of his underlings. He does not simply debase scientific thought; he uses something like science to stampede and persecute. Facetious lines like "Are you a Martian?" (100) become sinister when Thunderclap's paranoia gets to work. He subsumes all his political enemies and fantasies under the term *Martian*. "'The thing's out at last,' he said. 'Listen to him! Listen to what Rigamey has to tell us. We've been barking up the wrong tree. These Reds—Moscow—Bernard Shaw—New Dealers—Atheists—Protocols of Zion, all of that—mere agents. It's *Mars* that is after us" (103). The worst kind of discrimination is about to be let loose: "What he had in mind seemed to be some sort of worldwide witch-smelling for Martians everywhere. He swept aside every difficulty there might be in distinguishing them. You could tell them by the things they said and the way they behaved. You could tell them because *instinctively* you disliked them. . . . Not a massacre. Massacres were out of date. What was needed was a vast sanitary concentration of all these people to save our race (Lord Thunderclap) alive" (104). The ellipsis is in Wells's text. In that gap between instinctive dislike and massacre, a terrifying logic lurks. Here, in language that disturbingly anticipates Nazi anti-Semitism, is the final solution.

The dark vision is exaggerated from the start. Lord Thunderclap's staff bring him back down, and all returns to laughter, but not before we have had a glimpse of some of the potentials in this idea when made public, potentials that cannot be dismissed. Even as they discuss in the utopian isolation of Keppel's dining room the possibilities of the Martian change, Keppel, Holdman Stedding, and Davis can never "come out." They always hedge their assertions, and they always assure each other that they would never say these things outside of this very special place, this "palace of truth," the one place in which truth, not power, not possibility, is the only value.

If Davis is overly attached to the Martian idea, Professor Keppel, the closest thing in the novel to the voice of Wells himself, keeps the idea at a distance, always posing it as a hypothesis, a stimulant to utopian speculation. It is Keppel who insists on seeing the world without fantasy. "The last achievement of the human mind is to see life simply and see it whole" (118). And it is Keppel who briefly but graphically describes the crisis threatening the world, the "general effect of things going to pieces" (114). He diagnoses the dangers: "Assertive patriotism, mass fear, and the impulse to persecute—particularly the impulse to persecute—seem to me to be more dreadfully in evidence today that ever before in human affairs" (115). This last may be inspired by Thunderclap's paranoid revelation, but it also recalls "this stampeding of crowds which we call the course of history" (115), a description that causes Davis himself a moment of discomfort. And yet Keppel also voices the utopian hope that the Martians, "with their hard, clear minds and their penetrating, unrelenting questions stinging our darkness as the stars sting the sky" (117), will "salvage us," and he describes in very general terms what a "sane" world might be like. Nevertheless, though he entertains the idea, he slides away from the idea of hope depending on mutation to a more familiar Wellsian hope based on a radically serious and reformed education: "Isn't the time almost ripe for a new education that would clear the stuff from the creature's eyes, stiffen his backbone, teach him to think straight and grow up? Make a man of him at last" (120). The lovely ambiguity is that, even if this "creature" is something more than human—perhaps even "Martian"—its final apotheosis is to be transformed by education into "a man."

Kepple's skepticism about the Martian idea is evident throughout. He eyes Davis in such a way as to suggest that he is as interested in him as a specimen, an instance of a belief held with a passion that will not let him go, as much as a friend. If Davis is committed to the promise of "Martianized" minds solving the riddle of the future, Keppel's faith in that future depends less and less on genetic mutation. His language moves to terms like "our successors," "new-comers," "these heirs" (130). To Keppel's anguished "This life we might have had, instead of these mere compromises and consolations which make up life today," Dr. Holdman Stedding responds, "This would not be human life. This new world is something beyond all ordinary experience, something alien" (132), but he may not mean "Martian." A rational future would, whatever its source, be "alien" to people who have lived in the half-realized, frustrating world of today. Like the Eloi, as Wells had described them forty years earlier, future humans will not be "human" in our familiar sense, not because they have been tampered with or mixed with alien genes, but simply because they have evolved, whether through mutation or through education, to the point that we can no longer recognize them. It is the future itself that will be inevitably and by necessity alien—thanks in part, of course, to time and evolution, not by any special miracle of genetic manipulation. Even Davis in his final questions uses the ambiguous phrase, "these coming people" (120).

Keppel's last words to Davis emphasize the ambiguity of his position. He does not believe that the world "will go sane" (perhaps something different from going Martian?), but he at the same time does not disbelieve it (132). Wells has a long history of letting novels have it both ways. We recall that at the end of *The Time Machine* the narrator and the time traveler have antithetical visions of the possibilities of the human future: "I, for my own part, cannot think that these latter days of weak experiment, fragmentary theory, and mutual discord are indeed man's culminating time! I say, for my own part. He [i.e., the time traveler], I know—for the question had been discussed among us long before the Time Machine was made—thought but cheerlessly of the Advancement of Mankind, and saw in the growing pile of civilization only a foolish heaping that must inevitably fall back upon and destroy its makers in the end."[41] Such internal contradiction is simple, but it keeps in play mental complexity. The simple position is always false. Openness—to the future, to possibilities, and to disaster—is essential if we are going to address the enormous difficulties of the present situation.

Star Begotten closes by leaving us with a number of possibilities. Joseph Davis may be unreliable, even a little mad. But that does not end the story. He is under stress, and his vision of reality at the end, though fantastic, may, nevertheless, be a revealing, figurative rendering of the state of things. In this case, the idea that has been the subject of the novel from the beginning is most telling as an expression of the need for a utopian hope. After all, deluded or not, Davis has changed. Echoing his wife's startling earlier assertion that she has "done" with music, Davis can declare in the last chapter that he has "done with lullabies" (136). He has burnt the foolish and misleading book he was writing, and he plans to let his earlier, very profitable potboilers that promoted a simple and violent nationalism go out of print. Even if he has not become a Martian, he has at least become a Wellsian. This is a curious finale: we acknowledge the reasonableness of the need even as we doubt the reality of the process. Let us for the moment allow that Joseph Davis's fantasy could have a respectable motive.

In 1936, the year before he published Star Begotten, Wells wrote a short novel that performs explicitly just the sort of double reading I am tracing in Star Begotten. In the first chapters of The Croquet Player, young Dr. Finchatton tells Mr. Frobisher, the croquet player of the title, about a mysterious primitive evil emanating from rural Cainsmarsh. In his chilling and appalling narrative, Finchatton makes convincing the inexplicable despair under which the area lives. Then, abruptly, in the second half of the novel, Dr. Norbert, a psychologist treating Finchatton, appears and explains Finchatton's version of things as a fantasy constructed by a mind in distress as a way of hiding the even more threatening horrors of the real world crisis. This novel forces the re-reading of the first narrative as a delusion and gives an explanation for its ambiguity. The "real" in *The Croquet Player* is not the haunted marsh but the psychological stress associated with the larger world crisis. *Star Begotten* covers similar ground, but without the narrative instructions that by telling us what is "true" and what "delusion" save us from having to wrestle with the meaning ourselves. In *The Croquet Player* Wells tells us how to see and interpret delusion; in *Star Begotten* he has taken a step toward the more difficult style of his modernist colleagues and let the problem rest unexplained and unresolved.

Why should Wells so carefully maintain the suggestion that the Martian idea is compromised, even a delusion, that Keppel and Hold-man Stedding are never entirely serious, and that Davis himself is at bottom a foolish man? I would suggest that Wells is at a moment when he wants a rational solution—which the Martian invasion is not!—and he wants to debunk what he sees as the false utopias offered by fascism and communism. It is a threatening moment: when hope must always check itself and wonder if it is not gullibility; when crusades, thanks to the terrible example of the Nazis, need to be distrusted, but neverthe-less a moment when a crusade is badly needed. *Star Begotten* puts SF to a severe test by asking the reader both to follow a line of utopian thought with a parascientific idea behind it and at the same time to critique all arguments.

If SF is commonly overeager to embrace outlandish ideas, this novel makes sure that such an embrace should always be hesitant and alert to the misdirection they may entail. On the one hand, *Star Begotten* is a parodic renunciation of the imaginative basis of the scientific ro-mance. On the other, it is an acknowledgment that Wells's utopian ideals—expressed at the center of the novel by Professor Keppel—find an essential ground and energy in the scientific romance. With great simplicity and subtlety and with a seldom recognized carefulness of style that holds unclosed the questions about the validity of many as-sertions and the complexity of motive of the asserters, Wells has cre-ated a work of SF that allows for fantasy while at the same time insist-ing that the reader never abandon critical thought. This is a difficult tension that characterizes much of Wells's late work: we need to offer solutions unceasingly, but at the same time we need to be skeptical of solutions that are traps, that are dead ends that can't work, that are just childish hopes that someone will come to rescue us.

Star Begotten's taunting ambiguities, developed at the same time as Wells is writing such a polemical and exhortatory work as The Fate of Homo Sapiens, may have elements of the despair that will begin to eat at Wells in his final years. Kepple has declared, "Our social order is bankrupt. It is not delivering the goods. It is defaulting and breaking up" (114). The phrase "Leave not a rack behind," from Prospero's "Our revels now are ended" speech, which Kepple quotes in another pessimistic moment (132), would haunt Wells in his last years. In his final book, Mind at the End of Its Tether, Wells again quotes Prospero, this time when the world has declined beyond bankruptcy: "Our universe is not merely bankrupt; there remains no dividend at all; it has not simply liquidated; it is going clean out of existence, *leaving not a wracke behind*. The attempt to trace a pattern of any sort is absolutely futile."[42] When, in response to Kepple, Dr. Holdman Stedding pityingly remarks, "Poor Homo sapiens . . . is very near the end of its tether," he adumbrates The Fate of Homo Sapiens as it moves toward that despairing final book.[43] The Fate of Homo Sapiens speaks to that aspect of Wells/Keppel that still "believes" the promise of the myth of rational order, of "Martianizing" in whatever form, while Mind at the End of Its Tether represents that aspect which despairs of the future. Read this way, Star Begotten becomes a pivotal work in which we can see Wells playing with the antithetical possibilities that confront his world, hoping for a solution but at the same time mocking delusions.

In such a moment of crisis, Star Begotten marks an important balancing point: just as the rest of the world is establishing a formula of SF derived from his earlier scientific romances, he turns the genre toward self-reflection. Though most of the first reviewers tried to read the novel as a version of the genre they had come to expect, at least some, Olaf Stapledon and J. B. S. Haldane in particular, because they took the novel's issues very seriously, intuited the difficulties the novel raises. The novel's thorough ambiguity sets it apart from other science fiction with which we are familiar, and we can appreciate Wells's accomplishment by contrasting it with other lines of development in the genre at the time.

One strong line, pursued by many of SF's best-known talents, backs off from ambiguities altogether and attempts to render an unproblematic future world in exciting and bold detail. This is the direction that American pulp SF was to pursue over the next few decades with great energy. One might think of Robert Heinlein's "The Roads Must Roll" (1940), with its explicit reference to Wells's *When the Sleeper Wakes*, as a call to return to Wells's earlier adventure mode. Heinlein also, to be sure, changes radically the political values of Wells's imagery: the moving roads, which in Wells symbolize the oligarchy's control of the landscape and the oppression of labor, become in Heinlein a positive symbol whose vulnerability justifies strong, military control. But more important, though Heinlein's story may have some inner contradictions, on the surface it is an effort to write a work that is free from ambiguity.[44]

A second line features bold allegory and can be clearly observed in C. S. Lewis's space trilogy. The Wells that Lewis attacks explicitly a number of times in these novels is not the ambiguous author of *Star Begotten* but rather the antireligious utopian liberal. But again, for present purposes, we should appreciate how Lewis's strong religious allegory differs from the ironic and ambiguous possibilities for allegory we see in *Star Begotten*.[45]

There is, however, a third direction, one that has not received the attention it deserves, that may owe more to *Star Begotten* than is commonly acknowledged: the development of an ironic SF. Probably the most significant work to descend directly from Wells's novel is Stapledon's own novella, *The Flames* (1947), the subtitle of which, *A Fantasy*, recalls the subtitle of *Star Begotten*.[46] This relentlessly ambiguous tale consists of a manuscript written by an asylum inmate to his friend, a skeptic, in which the writer asks us to believe that creatures from the sun—not just Martians but star-begotten intelligences—who claim to have humanity's best interests in mind pose a great threat to the world. As in *Star Begotten*, the unanswered yet unavoidable question is whether the idea that shapes the narrative has any reality or not. The skeptical editor, who does not know how to resolve the truth of the warning, adds further layers to the ambiguity. Arthur C. Clarke would pursue a similarly ironic comedy in stories like "The Star" and "The Nine Billion Names of God," but without the disturbing sense that the fantasy raises questions about our own real future. Finally, in the 1950s in the United States, in the work of writers like Robert Sheckley, William Tenn, Kurt Vonnegut, and Philip K. Dick, a dark existentialist comedy develops that, different as it may be from Wells's socially explicit work, derives part of its generic heritage from Star Begotten. Delusion figures powerfully in this tradition. Sheckley in particular was obsessed with the psychological and disturbingly utopian possibilities of being taken over, invaded psychologically, by the alien.[47] On such a map of SF after 1940—American pulp romance, religious allegory, and ironic comedy—Star Begotten—a critique of the first two strains and the patron of the third—appears as a crucial text. In a time of impending world crisis, it poses a fantasy that asks to be challenged as fantasy even as it rallies the readership to the serious critical work that has to be done.

Note on the Text

This text of *Star Begotten* is based on the first U.K. edition, published in June 1937. It has been checked against the first U.S. edition, also June 1937 (cited as U.S.) and the three-installment serial publication in the *London Mercury* (cited below as LM; chapters 1–3 in vol. 35, no. 210, April 1937, 553–82; chapters 4–7 in vol. 36, no. 211, May 1937, 37–66; chapters 8–10 in vol. 36, no. 212, June 1937, 151–79).

Star Begotten has been printed three times in paperback: North Hollywood: Leisure Books, Inc., 1970; New York: Manor Books, Inc, 1975; London: Sphere Books, Ltd., 1975. All three texts, including the U.K. one, seem to be based on the U.S. edition. The U.K. paperback mistakenly proclaims itself the "First U.K. Publication."

The LM summaries at the beginning of each installment are interesting for their emphases and characterizations, and for what they omit and ignore. The following appears before the May 1937 installment:

> *The first instalment of this story appeared last month. It is concerned with an 'idea' which started in a scientific discussion at the Planetarium Club—an hypothesis that the Martians are capable of direct interference with the earth by imposing their form and character on our unborn children by means of cosmic rays. Mr. Joseph Davis, "a man of letters, a sensitive, intelligent and cultivated man," was peculiarly impressed by the idea. At the moment he was in a state of nervous tension, assailed by doubts of his early convictions, puzzled by the outlook and behaviour of his singular wife, and about to become a father. Applying the idea to his personal affairs, he has just taken Dr. Stedding, his wife's doctor, into his confidence.*

The third installment, June 1937, begins with this summary:

> *The third and concluding instalment of this story, which began in April. It is concerned with an "idea" which started in a scientific discussion at the Planetarium Club—an hypothesis that the Martians are capable of direct interfer-*

ence with the earth by imposing their form and character on our unborn children by means of cosmic rays. Mr. Joseph Davis, "a man of letters, a sensitive, intelligent, and cultivated man," was peculiarly impressed by the idea. At the moment he was in a state of nervous tension, assailed by doubts of his early convictions, puzzled by the outlook and behaviour of his singular wife, and about to become a father. Applying the idea to his personal affairs, he took Dr. Stedding, his wife's doctor, into his confidence. There was nothing abnormal about the birth of the child, but Dr Stedding encouraged Davis to carry out research among geniuses and misfits, and discussed the idea repeatedly with his friend Keppel, a psychotherapist. In a short time the "Martians" made their appearance in the newspapers and in political slogans.

It seems unlikely that Wells wrote either of these descriptions.

Aside from minor differences in spelling and the conventions of punctuation, the three editions are almost identical. All three editions set off quotations by using double quotation marks. Curiously, on page 129 the U.K. and London Mercury editions also use double quotation marks within a quotation, while at this point the U.S. edition employs the conventional single quotation marks. The following are differences that reveal some independent editorial choices, often quite slight:

Title: *Star Begotten* [*Star-Begotten* (U.S. and LM)]
Dedication [U.S. edition's dedication reads: "To my Friend / WINSTON SPENCER CHURCHILL." LM does not have a dedication.]
All characters in this Fantasia are fictitious [not in LM]
38. you must never never even think [must never even (U.S.)]
39. try and be a Mr [try to be a Mr (U.S.)]
42–43. he was for the show [he *was for* the show (LM)]
48. As though that mattered [not a separate line in LM]
49. The word is *fear* [the word is—*fear* (U.S.)]
50. You're telling me that," said [You're telling me that?" said (U.S.)]
51. He would say things [He could say things (LM)]
52. aesthetic enterprise. [End of paragraph (LM)]
52. assertion of an individuality; it was [assertion of an individuality? It was (LM)]
53. lovely to him, Mona Lisa [lovely to him. Mona Lisa (U.S.)]

57. "You say Tell me—and Tell me. ["You say 'Tell me'—and 'Tell me.' (LM)]

57. interrupt. [interrupt? (U.S.)]

62. "They come, I tell ye, from ["They come, I told you, from every (LM)]

64. "Nine hundred and ninety-nine per cent" ["Ninety-nine and nine-tenths per cent" (U.S.)]

67. anything in the way of out-of-the-way novelties (anything in the way—of out-of-the-way (U.S.)]

79. "Let's suppose it. I'm more ["Let's suppose it," said Keppel, "I'm more (LM)]

89. she's doing splendidly." [new paragraph] Whereupon Dr Holdman [she's doing splendidly." Whereupon Dr Holdman (U.S.)]

93. he asked, what is *spiritual?*" [he asked, 'what is *spiritual?*'" (LM)]

93. Why, he said should we make . . . primary opposites?" ['Why,' he said, 'should we make . . . primary opposites.'" (LM)]

97. *The Voice of the Stars* ["The Voice of the Stars," (U.S.)]

98. *The Fantastic Connexion of Cosmic Rays and Human Mutations* ["The Fantastic Connection of Cosmic Rays and Human Mutations" (U.S.)]

98. *The Martian Genes* ["The Martian Genes" (U.S.)]

98. *The Martian Type* ["The Martian Type" (U.S.)]

98. "Consider the," he expatiated, "—we will not say ["Consider the," he expatiated, "we will not say (LM); "Consider," he expatiated, "the—we will not say (U.S.)]

99. "In effect," said Mr Keppel ["In effect," said Professor Keppel (U.S.)]

99. the Resurrection and the end [the Resurrection of the Dead and the end (U.S.)]

100. The music-halls were brisk rather [The vaudeville stage was brisk (U.S.)]

101. endure this unprotesting acquiescence of the world [endure the unprotesting acquiescence of this world (U.S.)]

101. Most terrifyingly there [Most terrifying there (LM)]

101. What net were they weaving [a separate paragraph (LM)]

102. noses like foxes, needy [noses like foxes', needy (U.S.)]

108. said Mr Keppel, crouching [said Keppel, crouching (U.S.)]

113. they would have found themselves [they will have found themselves. (U.S.)]

113. They would have found a disconcerting [They will have found a disconcerting (U.S.)]

113. They would have thought at first [They will have thought at first (U.S.)]

113. They would have found themselves doubting [They will have found themselves doubting (U.S.)]

116. The B.B.C. would probably [The British Broadcasting Company would probably (U.S.)]

117. gathered his forces [new paragraph] "It's a half-born [gathered his forces. "It's a half-born (U.S.)]

138. among the piled manuscript [among the piled manuscripts. (U.S.)]

140. "M e !" he said at last. "Y o u t h i n k t h a t o f m e !" ["Me!" he said at last. "*You think that of me!*" (U.S.)]

141. THE END [not in U.S.]

Star Begotten
A Biological Fantasia
by H. G. Wells

Dedicated

On a Sudden Impulse

To My Friend[1]

WINSTON SPENCER CHURCHILL

All characters in this Fantasia

are fictitious

CHAPTER 1

The Mind of Mr Joseph Davis is Greatly Troubled

1

This is the story of an idea and how it played about in the minds of a number of intelligent people.

Whether there was any reality behind this idea it is not the business of the storyteller to say. The reader must judge for himself. One man believed it without the shadow of a doubt and he shall be the principal figure in the story.

Maybe we have not heard the last of this idea. It spread from the talk of a few people into the magazines and the popular press. It had a vogue. You certainly heard of it at the time though perhaps you have forgotten. Popular attention waned. Now the thing flickers about in people's minds, not quite dead and not quite alive, disconnected and ineffective. It is a queer and almost incredible idea, but yet not absolutely incredible. It is a bare possibility that this thing is really going on.

This idea arose in the mind of Mr Joseph Davis, a man of letters, a sensitive, intelligent, and cultivated man. It came to him when he was in a state of neurasthenia, when the strangest ideas may invade and find a lodgement in the mind.

2

The idea was born, so to speak, one morning in November at the Planetarium Club.

Yet perhaps before we describe its impact upon Mr Joseph Davis in the club smoking-room after lunch, it may be well to tell the reader a few things about him.

We will begin right at the beginning. He was born just at the turn of the century and about the vernal equinox. He had come into the world with a lively and precocious intelligence and his "quickness" had been the joy of his mother and his nurses. And, after the manner of our kind, he had clutched at the world, squinted at it, and then looked straight at it, got hold of things and put them in his mouth, begun to imitate, begun to make and then interpret sounds, and so developed his picture of this strange world in which we live.

His nurse told him things and sang to him; his mother sang to him and told him things, a nursery governess arrived in due course to tell him things, and then a governess and a school and a lot of people and pictures and little books in words of one syllable and then normal polysyllabic books and a large mellifluous parson and various husky small boys and indeed a great miscellany of people went on telling him things and telling him things. And so continually, his picture of this world, and his conception of himself and what he would have to do, and ought to do and wanted to do, grew clearer.

But it was only very gradually that he began to realize that there was something about his picture of the universe that perhaps wasn't in the pictures of the universe of all the people about him. On the whole the universe they gave him had an air of being real and true and just there and nothing else. There were, they intimated, good things that were simply good and bad things that were awful and rude things that you must never never even think of, and there were good people and bad people and simply splendid people, people you had to like and admire and obey and people you were against, people who were rich and prosecuted you if you trespassed and ran over you with motor cars if you did not look out, and people who were poor and did things for you for small sums, and it was all quite nice and clear and definite and you went your way amidst it all circumspectly and happily, laughing not infrequently.

Only—and this was a thing that came to him by such imperceptible degrees that at no time was he able to get it in such a way that he could ask questions about it—ever and again there was an effect as though this sure and certain established world was just in some elusive manner at this point or that point translucent, translucent and a little threadbare, and as though something else quite different lay behind it. It was never transparent. It was commonly nine days out of ten, a full, complete universe and then for a moment, for a phase, for a perplexing interval, it was as if it was a painted screen that hid—What did it hide?

They told him that a God of eastern Levantine origin, the God of Abraham (who evidently had a stupendous bosom) and Isaac and Jacob, had made the whole universe, stars and atoms, from start to finish in six days and made it wonderfully and perfect, and had set it all going and, after some necessary ennuis called the Fall and the Flood, had developed arrangements that were to culminate in the earthly happiness and security and eternal bliss of our Joseph, which had seemed to him a very agreeable state of affairs. And further they had shown him the most convincing pictures of Adam and Eve and Cain and Abel and had given him a Noah's Ark to play with and told him simple Bible stories about the patriarchs and the infant Samuel and Solomon and David and their remarkable lessons for us, the promise of salvation spreading out from the Eastern Levant until it covered the world, and he had taken it all in without flinching because at the time he had no standards of comparison. Anything might be as true as anything else. Except for the difference in colour they put him into the world of *Green Pastures*[2] and there they trained him to be a simply believing little Anglican.

And yet at the same time he found a book in the house with pictures of animals that were quite unlike any of the animals that frequented the garden of Eden or entered the Ark. And pictures of men of a pithecoid unpleasant type who had lived it seemed long before Adam and Eve were created. It seemed all sorts of things had been going on before Adam and Eve were created, but when he began to develop a curiosity about this pre-scriptural world and to ask questions about it his current governess snapped his head off and hid that disconcerting book away. They were "just antediluvian animals" she said, and Noah had not troubled to save them. And when he had remarked that a lot of them could swim, she told him not to try and be a Mr Cleverkins.

He did his best not to be Mr Cleverkins. He did his best to love this God of Abraham, Isaac and Jacob as well as fear him (which he did horribly, more even than he did the gorilla in Wood's *Natural History*)[3] and to be overcome with gratitude for the wisdom and beauty of a scheme of things which first of all damned him to hell-fire before he was born and then went to what he couldn't help thinking were totally unnecessary pains on the part of omnipotence to save him. Why should omnipotence do that? Why need He do that? All He had to do was just to say it. He had made the whole world by just saying it.

Master Joseph did his very best to get his feelings properly adjusted to the established conception of the universe. And since most of the scriptures concerned events that were now happily out of date, and since his mother, his governess, the mellifluous parson, the scripture teacher at school and everybody set in authority over him, converged in assuring him that now, at the price of a little faith and conformity, things were absolutely all right here and hereafter so far as he was concerned, he did get though some years pretty comfortably. He did not think about it too much. He put it all away from him—until the subtle alchemy of growth as he became adolescent sent queer winds of enquiry and correlation banging open again unsorted cupboards of his brain.

He went to St. Hobart's school and then to Camborne Hall, Oxford. There is much unreasonable criticism of the English public schools,[4] but it is indisputable that they do give a sort of education to an elect percentage of their boys. There was quite a lot of lively discussion at St. Hobart's in those days; it wasn't one of your mere games-and-cram schools, and the reaction against the dogmatic materialism[5] of the later nineteenth century was in full swing there. The head in his sermons and the staff generally faced up to the fact that there had been Doubt, and that the boys ought to know about it.

The science master was in a minority of one on the staff and he came up to St. Hobart's by way of a technical school;[6] the public school spirit cowed him. St. Hobart's did not ignore science but it despised the stuff, and all the boys were given some science so that they could see just what it was like.

Davis because of his mental quickness had specialized in the classical side; nevertheless he did his minimum of public school science. He burnt his fingers with hot glass and smashed a number of beakers during a brief interlude of chemistry, and he thought biology the worst of stinks. He found the outside of a rabbit delightful but the inside made him sick; it made him physically sick. He acquired a great contempt for "mere size" and that kept astronomy in its place. And when he came to grips with doubt, in preparation for confirmation,[7] he realized that he had been much too crude in feeling uncomfortable about that early Bible narrative and the scheme of salvation and all the rest of it. As a matter-of-fact statement it was not perhaps in the coarser sense true, but that was because of the infirmities of language and the peculiar low state of the eastern Levantine intelligence and eastern Levantine moral ideas when the hour to "reveal" religion had struck. Great resort had had to be made for purposes of illustration to symbols, parables, and inaccurate but edifying stories. People like David and Jacob had been poor material for demonstration purposes, but that was a point better disregarded.

The story of creation was symbolical and its failure to correspond with the succession of life on earth did not matter in the least, the Fall was symbolical of things too mysterious to explain, and why there had to be an historical redemption when the historical fall had vanished into thin air was the sort of thing no competent theologian would dream of discussing. There it was. Through such matters of faith and doctrine Joseph Davis was taken at a considerable speed, which left him hustled and baffled rather than convinced.

But the curious thing about these initiatory explanations was, that all the time another set of ideas at an entirely different level was being put before him as a complete justification for the uncritical acceptance of Bible, Church and Creed. It was being conveyed to him that it really did not matter what foundations of myth or fantasy the existing system of western civilization was built upon; the fact that mattered was that it was built upon that foundation and that a great ritual of ceremonial and observance which might be logically unmeaning, and an elaborate code of morality which might ultimately prove to be arbitrary, nevertheless constituted the co-ordinating fabric of current social life and that social life could not now go on without them. So that all this free-thinker and rationalist stuff became irrelevant and indeed contemptibly crude. Reasonable men didn't assert. They didn't deny. There were thinking and living at a different level. You could no more reconstruct religion, social usage, political tradition, than you could replan the human skeleton—which also was open to considerable criticism.

That put Joseph Davis in his place. Arguments about the Garden of

Eden and Jonah's Whale passed out of discussion. He was left face to face with history and society. Christianity and its churches, the monarchy and political institutions, the social hierarchy, seemed to be regarding him blandly. It is no good inquiring into our credentials now, they seemed to say. Here we are. We work. (They seemed to be working then.) And what other reality is there?

By this time he was at Oxford, talking and thinking occasionally, pretending to think a lot and believing that he was thinking a lot. The dualism that had dawned upon him in childhood looked less like being resolved than ever. The world-that-is no longer contested his fundamental criticisms, but it challenged him to produce any alternative world-that-might-be. There it was, the ostensible world, definite, fundamentally inconsistent maybe, but consistent in texture. An immense accumulation of falsity and yet a going concern. So things are.

It looked so enduring. He wavered for a time. On one hand was the brightly lit story of current things, the front-window story, a mother's-knee story of a world made all for his reception, a world of guidance, safe government, a plausible social order, institutions beyond effective challenge, a sure triumph for good behaviour and a clear definition of right and wrong, of what was done and what was not done, and against it was no more than a shadow story which was told less by positive statement than by hints, discords that stirred beneath the brightness, murmurs from beneath and vague threats from incidental jars. That shadow world, that mere criticism of accepted things, had no place for him, offered him nothing. No shapes appeared there but only interrogations. The brightly lit story seemed safest, brightest and best to his ripening imagination; he did his best to thrust that other tale down among all sorts of other things, improper and indecent thoughts for example, that have to be kept under hatches in the mind.

Momentous decisions have to be made by all of us in those three or four undergraduate years; we take our road, and afterwards there is small opportunity for a return. Mr Joseph Davis had a quick mind and a facile pen and he was already writing, and writing rather well, before he came down. He chose to write anyhow. His father had left him with a comfortable income and there was no mercenary urgency upon him. He elected to write about the braver more confident aspects of life. He was for the show. He began to write heartening and stalwart books and to gird remorselessly at dissidence and doubt. What I write, he said, shall have banners in it and trumpets and drums. No carping, nothing subversive. Sociology is going out of fashion. So he committed himself. He began first with some successful, brave historical romances and followed up with short histories of this or that gallant interlude in the record.

King Richard and Saladin was his first book and then he wrote *The Singing Seamen*. Then came *Smite with Hammer, Smite with Sword*, and after that he ran up and down the human tree, telling of the jolly adventures of Alexander and Caesar and Jenghis Khan (*The Mighty Riders*) and the Elizabethan pirates and explorers and so on. But as he had a sound instinct for good writing and an exceptionally sensitive nature, the more he wrote, the more he read and learnt and—which was the devil of it—thought.

He should not have thought. When he took his side he should, like a sensible man, have stopped thinking.

Besides which some people criticized him rather penetratingly, and for an out-and-out champion he was much too attentive to criticism.

He became infected with a certain hesitation about what he was doing. Perhaps he was undergoing that first subtle deterioration from that assurance of youth which is called "growing up"; a phase that may occur at any age. He wrote with diminishing ease and confidence and let qualifying shadows creep into his heroic portraits. He would sometimes admit quite damaging things, and then apologize. He found this enhanced the solidity of some of his figures, but it cast a shadow on his forthright style. He told no one of this loss of inner elasticity, but he worried secretly about it.

Then, courageously but perhaps unwisely, he resolved to make a grand culminating frontal attack upon the doubt, materialism and pessimism of shadowland, in the form of a deliberately romanticized history of mankind.[8] It was to be a world history justifying the ways of God to man.[9] It was also to justify his own ways to himself. It was to be a great parade—a cavalcade of humanity.

For some reason he never made clear to himself, he did not begin at the creation of the world but on the plain of Shinar.[10] He put the earlier history into the mouths of retrospective wise old men. From the Tower of Babel man dispersed about the world.

History regarded with a right-minded instinct has often a superficial appearance of being only a complicated tangle still awaiting analysis, and it was not always easy to show Man winning all the time and Right for ever triumphant against the odds—in the long run, that is. *The Heritage of Mankind, the Promise and the Struggle*—that was one of the titles he was considering—implies a struggle with, among other things, malignant fact. Fact sometimes can be very obstinate and malignant.

He had got himself into a tangle with the Black Death. He had started—rashly, he was beginning to realize—upon a chapter dealing with the ennobling effect of disease, one of three to be called respectively, *Flood, Fire* and *Pestilence*; and that had led him into a considerable amount of special reading. He had always been for taking his own where he found it, and he had been inspired by Paul de Kruif's *Microbe Hunters*[11] to annex some of that writer's material, infuse it with religious devotion, and then extend his discourse to show how throughout the ages these black visitations properly regarded had been glorious stimulants (happily no longer urgently needed) for the human soul. But he found the records of exemplary human behaviour during the Black Death period, disconcertingly meager. The stress was all on the horror of the time, and when everything was said and done our species emerged, hardly better in its reactions than a stampede of poisoned rats. That at any rate was how the confounded records showed things. And this in spite of his heroic efforts to read between the lines and in spite of his poetic disposition to supplement research with a little invention—intuition let us say, rather than invention. That he knew was a dangerous disposition. Too much intuition might bring down the disparagement of some scholarly but unsympathetic pedant upon him, and all the other fellows would be only too glad to pick it up and repeat it.

And then suddenly his mind began to slip and slide. He had, he realized, been overworking and what is so common an aspect of overwork, he could not leave off. Overwork had brought worry and sleeplessness in its train. He would lie awake thinking of the Black Death and the pitiful behaviour to which tormented humanity can sink. Vivid descriptive phrases in the old records it would have been healthier to forget, recurred to him. At first it was only the Black Death that distressed him and then his faith in human splendour began to collapse more widely. A cracked handbell heralded an open cart through the streets of plague-stricken London and once more the people were called upon to bring out the dead. Something revived his memory of the horror pictures of Goya in the Prado, and that dragged up the sinister paintings in the Wiertz Museum in Brussels.[12] That again carried him to the underside of Napoleon's career and the heaped dead of the Great War. Why write a *Grand Parade of Humanity*, asked doubt, when Winwood Reade has already written *The Martyrdom of Man*?[13] He found himself criticizing his early book about Alexander the Great, *Youth the Conqueror.*

He had told that story triumphantly. Now in the black morning hours, it came back upon him in reverse. Something in his own brain confronted him and challenged him. Your Alexander, it said, your great Alexander, the pupil of Aristotle, who was, as you say, the master mind of the world, was in truth, as you know, just an ill-educated spendthrift. Why do you try to pervert the facts? By sheer accident—and most history is still a tale of accidents—he found himself in a rotten, nerveless, self-indulgent world that had no grown men in it able to hold him out and give him the spanking he deserved, and as luck would have it, he had the only up-to-date and seasoned army in existence, completely at his disposal. He hadn't made it. It came to him. The fools went where he told them to go. When you wrote all that stuff about his taking Greek civilization to Persia and Egypt and India, you were merely giving him credit for what had happened already. Why? Greek civilization owed nothing to him. He took advantage of it. He picked it up and smashed it over the head of poor old Darius. Smashed it—just as these plunging dictators of today seem likely to smash your poor civilization—nobody able to gainsay them. He left the Glory that was Greece in fragments, for the Romans to pick up in their turn. He wasted the Macedonian cavalry and phalanx, just as our fools today are going to waste aviation.[14] For no good at all; for no plain result. Alexander was just a witless accident in an aimless world. And think of his massacres and lootings and how it fared with the women and children, the common life of the world. Why did you write this florid stuff about Alexander the Great?

And about Caesar—and about all these other pitiful heroes of mankind? Why do you keep it up, Joseph? If you did not know better then, you know better now. Your newspapers should be teaching you. Why do you pretend that a sort of destiny was unrolling? That it was all leading up to Anglicanism, cricket, the British Empire and what not? Why do you go on with these pretences? These great men of yours never existed. The human affair is more intricate than that. More touching. Saints are sinners and philosophers are fools. Religions are rigmaroles. If there is gold it is still in the quartz. Look reality in the face. Then maybe something might be done about it.

He got up. He walked about his room.

"But I thought I had settled all this years ago," he said. "How can I get on with *Grand Parade of Humanity* if I give way to this sort of thing? Already I have spent nearly a year on this overwhelming book."

He felt like some ancient hermit assailed by diabolical questionings. But that ancient hermit would at least have prayed and made the sign of the cross and got over it.

In his solitude Mr Joseph Davis tried that. But on his knees he had a frightful sense of play-acting. He didn't believe there was a hearer. He didn't believe that anyone believes nowadays—not Cantuar, not Ebor, not the Pope.[15] These old boys eased down on their knees out of habit and let their minds wander along a neglected familiar lane to find nothing in particular.

He got up again with his prayer half said and sat staring at the situation. *Defensor Fidei!*[16] He couldn't pray.

3

But this peculiar feeling of—mental duplicity shall we call it?—this doubt of himself; this struggle to sustain the clear bright assurance of his chosen convictions, was not the only strain upon Mr Davis's serenity. Several other matters not directly connected with his literary work were also conspiring to disturb his abnormally sensitive mind.

As he walked down Lower Regent Street from Piccadilly Station towards his club, various discontents, new ones and old ones, threaded their way round and about each other, each rasping against him and eluding him, dodging down into the subconscious and giving place to another whenever he tried to challenge it. The day was grey and over-cast and it gave him no help—was indeed definitely against him. He was inclined to think he would have been wiser to have put on his medium coat rather than his thin Burberry, and at the same time he found the air moist and stuffy.

Chief among these accessory troubles was this, that for the first time in his life he was to become a father. It is an occasion few men face with absolute calm; it stirs up all sorts of neglected or unexplored regions of possibility in the mind. No psycho-analyst as yet has investigated the imaginative undercurrents in the mind of the expectant father. No one has attempted a review of the onset of parentage in the male.[17] Here we must confine our attention strictly to the case of Mr Joseph Davis. For some time he had been developing a curious vague perplexity about this wife of his, who was so soon to add the responsibilities and anxieties of fatherhood to his already febrile mental activities, and that expectation had greatly intensified this perplexity.

Here again the subtle sensitiveness of the imaginative temperament came in. A literary man carries about with him in his head a collection of edged tools known as his Vocabulary. And sometimes he cuts himself. Two or three years ago "enigmatical" had, so to speak, stuck up suddenly and caught him when he was thinking about his wife. And "fey." She was fifteen years younger than he was, he had married her when she was scarcely more than a girl, and yet, he had been compelled to realize, she was enigmatical, extremely enigmatical.

To begin with he had loved her in a simple, straightforward, acquisitive way and she had seemed to love him. He had not thought about her very much; he had just loved her as a man loves a woman. Their early married life, subject to the obvious discretions of our time, had been natural and happy; she had learned to type for him and they had been inseparable and all that sort of thing. Then by imperceptible degrees things had seemed to change. His satisfaction in her clouded over. She had seemed to disentangle herself from him and draw herself together. More and more was he aware of a lack of response in her.

And then came the memorable evening when she had remarked: "I don't know whether I care for very much more of this sort of thing unless I am going to have a child."

47

This sort of thing! Roses, raptures, whispers, dusk, moonlight, nightingales, all the love poetry that ever was—*this sort of thing!*

So that was it!

"You are quite well off," she said.

As though that mattered. . . .

There had been a certain amount of argument, in which delicacy had prevailed over explicitness, and then she had carried her point. He had made it plain to her that whatever reluctance he might have displayed at first was solely on her account and that now they were embarked together on a shining adventure. They were to make life "more abundant." Once the proposal was accepted his imagination seemed to bubble offspring. He buried "this sort of thing" as deeply as he could under high-piled flower-beds of philoprogenitive sentiment; he tried his utmost to forget her strangely inhuman phrase.

Yet after everything was settled, still his uneasiness deepened, still her detachment seemed to increase.

It *seemed* to increase. But that was where another queer worry came now into his mind. Had she always had some or all of this disposition towards detachment, and had he failed to observe it hitherto? In the first bright months or so of their married life, when he had looked at her and she had looked at him their eyes had met upon a common purpose as if they were smacking hands together. But now it was as if her hand had become a phantom hand that his own hand went right through, and his gaze seemed always just to miss meeting her deep regard. Her dark eyes had become inaccessible. "Unfathomable" the vocabulary threw up. She scrutinized him and revealed nothing. Husbands and wives ought to become more easy with each other, more familiar, as life goes on, but she was increasingly aloof.

The majority of discontented husbands, the burthen of comic literature, proverbial wisdom, testify to the terrors of a talkative wife, but indeed these terrors are nothing to those of a silent woman, a silent thoughtful woman. A scolding wife can say endless disconcerting things and she hits or misses, but a silent woman says everything.

Always nowadays she seemed to be thinking him over. And his morbidly sensitive self-consciousness filled her silences with criticisms against which he had no defence.

When he had married her, a young, dark, shy girl, he had radiated protective possession all over her. It would have seemed impossible then that he should ever feel—it is a strange word to use about a wife and as we use it here we use it in its most sublimated and attenuated sense, but the word is *fear*. Latterly his uneasiness with his wife and about his wife had increased almost to the quality of that emotion.

Of course he had always realized that there was something subtly unusual about her, even about her appearance. But at first he had found that simply attractive. She was neither big nor clumsy but she was broadly built; her brow was broad and her dark grey eyes were unusually wide apart; the corners of her full mouth drooped gravely and at times he had a way of moving that was, so to speak, absentminded, preoccupied. At first he had valued all this as "distinction," but later he had come rather to think of her as "unusual." She was far more unusual than the faint foreignness of her Scotch origin and the slow deliberation of her speech justified her in being.

He had never liked her people, which was odd because he had hardly seen anything of them. She had come into his world as it seemed at first, romantically. He had met her at a publisher's cocktail party; she had been invited there rather for her ambitions than her performance, and she had told him then that her people lived in the Outer Hebrides and that they opposed her wish to study and write. She had just spoken of them as "people." She had won scholarships at a Glasgow high school, she had got to the university and so worked her way to London in defiance of them. She had written poetry, she told him, and she wanted to see it printed.

But London, she said, wasn't quite what she had expected it to be. London astonished, frightened and stimulated her, and kept on seeming stranger and stranger. She was not growing accustomed to it. People were always saying and doing the most unaccountable things.

"At times," she said, "I feel like a stray from another world. But then, you know, I felt very much the same when I was at home in the islands where I was born. Have you ever had that feeling? All you people here seem so sure of your world and of yourselves."

It was when she said this, that the idea of guiding this quiet, unsure and lovely young stranger to all the braveries of life entered the head of Mr Joseph Davis. It was so exceptional to meet an intelligent young woman who seemed unsure of herself and who was willing to be taught and hadn't already, in an irrational hurry to begin, taken the braveries of life to herself in her own fashion. It was not so much a candid inviting white virginity as an elusive elfin one she had. Here, he thought, was something fine and unformed to mould and shape and write flourishes upon.

He went about thinking of her more and more, with all those exploratory impulses aroused in him which constitute falling in love. He was soon completely in love with her.

When he offered to read some of her verse, she said she didn't want it read, she just wanted to see it in print and read it herself. When at last he saw it he liked it. It was like a missionary's translations from the Chinese; mostly vivid little word pictures. From the point of view of publication and running the gauntlet of all these modern poets and reviewers who cut you up with one hand and cut you out with the other, he did not think it likely to be successful. But it had nevertheless a curious simplicity, a curious directness and a faint wistful flavour.

He learnt that she was living in a students' hostel in Bloomsbury, he established contacts with her and he was able to take her about very freely. Perhaps at one time he had thought simply of becoming her first lover, but she had an unobtrusive defensiveness that made marriage the only way to her.

Two rawboned fishermen in bonnets and broadcloth suddenly appeared in London to "take a look at him" when the marriage was mooted. They were the most astonishing and unexpected "people" for her to produce. They had her dark colouring and dark grey eyes like hers, but otherwise they were singularly unlike her. Brawny they were. They had none of her manifest fineness and restraint.

"You'll have to take great care of her," they told him, "for she's been the treasure of our eyes. She's better than we and we know it. Why we ever let her persuade us that she had to come on to London is more than we can explain, but the mischief's been done and you've got her."

"She's lovely. You're telling me that," said Davis, and the elder brother, darkly reproachful, said "Aye. We're telling you."

They stayed in London until the wedding, and entertaining them was a little like making hay with seaweed. They seemed to keep on looking at him and passing Hebridean judgements on him. They were full of unspoken things.

He would say things to them and they would say "Eh"—just "Eh." Not an interrogative "Eh?" but an ambiguous acknowledgment.

They got drunk in a dutiful, dubious, and melancholy way for the registry office, and the last he saw of them was on the platform at Victoria when he carried her off to show her the wonders of Paris. They were standing together grave and distrustful, not gesticulating nor waving good-bye but each holding up a great red hand as who should say "We're here."

And when the last curve hid them and he pulled up the carriage window and turned to her to meet the love-light in her eyes she said to him: "And now you are going to show me the real world and all those cities and lakes and mountains where at last we shall feel at home."

Only she never did seem to feel at home.

She never talked about this family of hers to him, after the transit of these two samples, and she corresponded with them with an infrequent regularity. She never gave him any reason to suppose she cared very much for them. But the fact which presently became apparent that, unlike him, she was a good sailor and loved wind and rough seas, seemed to link her to them rather than to him. Many husbands have objected to their wives' relations because they were too near, but he found he objected to hers because they were too remote. And also she loved mountains and crags and precipitous places. He didn't. They climbed the Matterhorn at great expense; he gave more trouble to the guides than she did, and at the summit she seemed to be pleased but still gravely looking for more.

Once on holiday in Cornwall they had been basking together on the beach after lunch and suddenly her pose, as she sat thinking, reminded him of a picture he had seen somewhere of Undine, La Motte Fouqué's Undine,[18] sweet and detached, looking across the far levels of the sea, lost in some unimaginable reverie. Undine too had had some uncouth and menacing brothers. That was when the fancy of her as a sort of changeling, as something ultra-terrestrial and not quite human first came to him. That was when "fey" came out of the vocabulary.

This Undine suggestion hung about for months. First he let this exaggeration of her faint unearthliness play mischievously in his mind, and then he tried to restrain and banish it. Sometimes he tried to persuade himself that every man's wife is really an Undine, but he could never make really convincing observations in that matter. Maybe, he thought, you never get near enough to any woman but your own wife to appreciate her remoteness.

A multitude of possibly quite accidental divergences grouped themselves about that "fey."

He spun the thread of that word's suggestion into a web about her. It swept aside the one worse alternative that conceivably she was just simple and lacking in aesthetic enterprise. At first that "fey" was a fantastic exaggeration and then it became more and more an observation, an explanation for her undeniable detachment from so much that excited and stirred him, and from so much that he believed ought to excite and stir anybody. That struggle of his ideals with a dark underworld of doubts, which made it urgent for him to keep thinking, feeling, appreciating—like an urgent skater over thin ice and a cold abyss of disbelief—had no counterpart. She could keep still and remain content in her convictions, in something deep—whatever it was that she knew and did not communicate.

There was no malice in her detachment from him. He could have understood malice better. He had seen mutual jealousy and mutual detraction often enough among his married friends. The better the artists the worse the lovers. He understood that fight for individual assertion which makes love a legendary unreality, a blend of fantasy and grossness, in the world of the intelligentsia. But this was not the assertion of an individuality; it was a complete indifference to his values. It was a foreignness—to the whole world.

Whenever Mr Davis had a slump in his vitality he realized this widening estrangement from his wife more acutely. The lower the ebb the intenser the realization. And this day his realization was exceptionally vivid. . . .

This very morning she had made a remark that stirred him to a protest he abandoned in despair. There was to be a big concert at the Pantechnicon Hall with Rodhammer[19] conducting. He was enthusiastic for going. She did not want to go.

He argued against her disinclination. "You used to like music."

"But I have *heard* music, dearest."

"*Heard* music! My dear, what a queer way to put things!"

She shook her head from side to side without speaking. There was a time when the self-assurance of her faint smile had seemed very lovely to him, Mona Lisa and all that, but now it irritated him with a sense of invincible and unapproachable opposition.

"But you've only heard Rodhammer once before!"

"Why should I want to hear Rodhammer again—a little better or not so good?"

"But music!"

"There's a limit to music," she said.

"A limit!"

"I've a feeling that I've done with music. It was wonderful, charming, sustaining, all that music we went to hear—to begin with. I loved that as much as I've loved anything. But if one has taken music in— hasn't one taken it in?"

"Taken it in! You mean—?" he tried.

"I mean you don't always want to be sitting down to attend to it after you've heard—what there is of it. We aren't—professional."

Professional! When she did use words she used them in a very deadly fashion. "I never tire of music," he said.

"But does the sort of music there is say anything—does it say anything fresh?"

"It's eternally fresh."

"How?"

He made a hopeless gesture. "But why have you become indifferent?"

"But why are you still so enthusiastic?"

"But don't you get—something wonderful? An exaltation? A world of absolute sensuous emotion?"

"No—I did at first. A sort of exaltation. I agree. And still I like— rhythm. It's pleasant to hear music going on, but it's no longer something I want to listen to *specially*. Going to hear music in concerts seems to me like going to see pictures in galleries. . . . Or reading anthologies. . . . Or looking over a collection of butterflies in a museum. . . . A time comes . . ."

"Then, in short, you won't go to the concert?"

"I feel a little tired but I will go if you like."

"Oh! Not like *that*," he said and ended their talk.

But he went over it again in his own mind and now he was going over it once more. He knew people to whom music meant much and people to whom music meant little, but to take up music as Mary had, in a spirit of glad discovery, and then to put it down again as one might put down an unimportant novel, distressed his mind. But that was how she seemed to deal with everything in life. Even with friendship, even with love, she had that same flash of interest, that rapid appreciation, and then she turned away. To what?

He spoke aloud, addressing Lower Regent Street: "You can't *afford* to give up music like that. You can't *afford* to give up art."

And what he did not say because he could not bring himself to say it was "And how can you afford to give up love?"

When the child comes, will she give up that?

Or will she go on loving the child. Leaving me behind? My part played?

This eternal going on! This complete instability of values! . . .

Could it fail to distress a man who was in effect a professor of stable values?

4

And here we must note another rather unusual element in the *mélange* of Mr Davis's troubles, a queer little thing that would have mattered nothing to a less imaginative man, but which was to thread through all the train of thought upon which he was presently to embark. It was a very slender thread indeed, a matter so irrational and ridiculous that it seems almost unfair to him to mention it. And yet it certainly played a slight deflecting rôle in guiding him to the strange idea. It cannot therefore be ignored altogether.

Since his school days he had had a secret detestation of his own

Christian name. Facetious upper school boys had made it plain that there was a shadow on it. Neither in the Old Testament nor in the New, is the name of Joseph adorned with that halo of triumphant virility which is the desire of every young male.[20] He had struggled to insist that he should always be called "Jo." But the mortifying realization that he was a "Joseph" damped his private meditation.

There is not the faintest circumstance to justify any marital uneasiness on his part. No one sane could have entertained a suspicion of his Mary's integrity—nor did he, in the foreground of his mind. And yet, he would have been happier under a different name.

So it was.

5

Such were the ruling factors in the weak hotch-potch of thoughts and half-thoughts, fancies, suggestions, dream scraps and almost completely unsymbolized feelings, that circled in his mind on his way to the pillared portals of the Planetarium Club and his first encounter with this strange idea that was destined to stab through his imagination like a dagger and work a revolution in his life.

CHAPTER 2

Mr Joseph Davis Learns about Cosmic Rays

1

The Planetarium club abounds in unexpected conversations. It has a core of scientific men who are mostly devotees of the exact sciences, grave, shy, precise men, but wrapped round them are layers of biologists, engineers, explorers, civil servants, patent lawyers, criminologists, writers, even an artist or so. Almost any subject may be started in the smoking-room where most of the talk goes on, but the feeling against chewed newspaper is strong. Mr Davis, as he ascended the club steps, made an effort to throw off those vague shadows that oppressed his mind, and to brighten his bearing to the quality that may be reasonably expected of a temperamental optimist.

But as he recrossed the hall from the vestiary to the dining-room he was still undecided whether he should sit at one of the small tables and go on with his state of uneasy deterioration, or take a place at one of the sociable boards. He elected for solitude, but repented as soon as his decision was made, and after his solitary lunch he made a real effort at sociability and joined a talking circle of a dozen men or more between the window and the fire, sitting down next to Foxfield, that hairy, untidy biologist, for whom he had a slightly condescending liking. The talk was rather under the stress of a new member, a parliamentary barrister, who might be almost anything in a few years' time and manifestly felt as much. The man had been elected before it was realized that he was slightly larger than any one else in the club and disposed to behave accordingly, and his conversational method was rather an elucidatory cross-examination than an original contribution to the interchanges.

"Tell me," he would say and even point a finger. "I don't know anything about these things. Tell me—"

"Tell me," except in the case of monarchs, heirs-apparent, and presidents of the United States, is by the standards of the Planetarium, atrocious conversational manners. But so far no one in the club had been able to get this point of view over to the new-comer. It would happen sooner or later but so far it had not happened. He was talking now with an air of making out some sort of case against modern physics and demonstrating how entirely more sensible and practical a mind which had passed through the ennobling exercises of Greats[21] and a straight-forward legal and political training, could be.

"Atoms and force were good enough for Lucretius[22] and they were good enough for my stinks[23] master when I was a boy. Then suddenly you have to disturb all that. There's wonderful discoveries, and the air is full of electrons and neutrons and positions."

"Positrons," a voice corrected.

"It's all the same to us. Positrons. And photons and protons and deutrons. Alpha rays and Beta rays and Gamma rays and X rays and Y rays. And they fly about like solar systems and all the rest of it. And the dear old Universe, that used to be fixed and stable begins to expand and contract—like God playing a concertina. Tell me—frankly. I suggest to you—it's a Bluff. It's something out of nothing. It's just a way of selling us mystery bottles with scientific labels. I ask you."

He paused with the air of a man who has put a poser.

A small, elderly, but still acutely acid old gentleman was sitting deep in one of the arm-chairs. The finger had not challenged him, but now he put out a lean hand and spoke with a thin penetrating voice, like a rapier, with the faint glint of a Scotch accent along the edge.

"You say Tell me—and Tell me. Will you have the grace to listen while I tell ye? And not interrupt."

And when the slightly outsize member made as if he had something further to say, the old gentleman just raised his hand and said: "No. Listen, I tell ye, and told you shall be."

The rising man, just faintly abashed, assumed an attitude of skep-tical and slightly impatient intelligence, looking round the group for support in what he evidently imagined was going to be a duel of wits. Just for a moment he imagined that. And then suddenly he felt like fac-ing twelve implacably hostile jurymen and the first lesson of the Plane-tarium Club entered into his soul. Not to bounce.[24]

Quietly and unobtrusively he allowed himself to lapse into the pose of the modest best boy in the class who knows that he still has much to learn and who cannot command any one to tell him but is glad to be told.

"These things boil down," said the old gentleman. "I've lectured about them for years. And followed the changes. When one gets old one has to be concise and it's fortunate I've had some practice in packing my statements. Still I'll have to take five minutes. I'll do all I can for you. Those Oxford teachers of yours—for it's Oxford you come from—probably left your mathematical philosophy in a worse state than they found it when you came up from your English public school—if indeed your formula-dodging schoolmasters gave you any mathematical understanding at all even there—so I may not be able to *explain* everything to you. Some bits I'll just have to *tell* you—*as* you put it. But it's really quite simple and credible stuff they've made of it in the last twenty-five years, Rutherford and Bragg and Niels Bohr and the rest of those fellows,[25] and the younger people find no difficulty about it at all."

And with that and a galling air of careful simplification he proceeded to unfold a compact modern view of space and time and the movements of things therein. "Don't ask me what electricity is," he said, "and I'll tell you everything else as we have it up to date. It's none so complicated as you think and there's never a contradiction."

And very neatly he took his nucleus, twisted up his atoms with electrons and neutrons round the central proton, and sent them eddying into a world of throbbing photons. Then he ran his hand along the sixty-odd octaves of the spectrum from the hundred-yard electro magnetic undulations beyond the longest radio length through heat rays and light rays to X rays and Gamma rays, smacked a few atoms together, shot them through with helium atoms and described the results, and by way of epilogue gave a lucid word to those flying sub-atomies, the cosmic rays.

"After all, it's none so confused," he said, and indeed the pictures that arose as one listened to his slightly remonstrating very persuasive Scotch intonation, had the music of ripples and wavelets, of dancing reflections upon the side of a ship, of the concentric colour rings of films on water, of every sort of pleasant patterning and logical ornamentation. He made dead matter dance and circle, set to partners, interfere, shimmer, glow, become iridescent and mysteriously endowed with energy. The atoms of our fathers seemed by contrast like a game of marbles abandoned in a corner of a muddy playground on a wet day. He even had a cautious word for the young neutrinos, the latest aspirants to this dance in the atomic assembly rooms.[26] The one or two men who were experts in the subject listened, pleased to hear the A B C of their subject so lucidly delivered, and the rest were glad to check up their vague impressions of these fluctuating modern conceptions.

"And where do we come in?" asked someone. "Where is thought and the soul in all this?"

"Just a film, just a thin zone of reflection half-way in the scale of size between those electrons and the stars."

2

Davis followed that compact discourse in a mood of unusual self-forgetfulness. It was, he found, as refreshing as good drink, and as little likely to linger in the system. And even the new member betrayed a certain humility in his attention.

But he still felt it was his duty to himself to talk.

"Those cosmic rays of yours," he said. "They are the most difficult part of your story. They aren't radiations. They aren't protons. What are they? They go sleeting through the universe incessantly, day and night, going from nowhere to nowhere. For the life of me I find that hard to imagine."

"They must come from *somewhere*," said a quiet little man with an air of producing a very special contribution to the discussion.

"We note their existence," said the old gentleman. "We watch them but we draw no premature conclusions. They are infinitesimal particles flying at an inconceivable velocity. They come from all directions of outer space. And that's as much as we know about them. If I put out my finger like that for a second or so, there's only just a dozen or so gone through it in a second. And no harm done. Which is just as well. There's more up above us in the outer atmosphere. But fortunately they get reflected and absorbed. You know we have a sort of filtering halo about the earth, a sort of cloak of electrons, which keeps off any excess of these radiations."

"That Heaviside layer," a stout rufous man,[27] who had apparently been asleep, interpolated.

"And what may that be?" asked the barrister.

"It's a beautiful sample of scientific terminology," said the stout rufous man still somnolently. "This Heaviside layer, so far as I can understand it, is called so, because firstly it isn't heavy, secondly it hasn't any side and thirdly it is almost as much a layer as—as a rheumatic chill or a glow of indignation. Go on, Professor."

His eyes which had been partly open, closed again.

"You said," said the examining barrister, "that *fortunately* they are kept off. *Why*—fortunately? May I ask?"

"My thankfulness may have been a little unwarranted," said the old gentleman. "But these cosmic rays have a lot of energy, considering their size. They knock atoms about when they hit them. And we and our belongings are made of atoms. A lot of them, a great lot of them, a real douche of cosmic rays, might cause all sorts of tissue diseases, blow up mines, strike the matches in our pockets. But as it is they don't often hit even *one* atom—quantitatively they're more ineffective even than that infinitesimal quantity of radiation that is always coming up from the radium in the earth; and so Nature is able to clean up any little speck of mess that occurs."

"Not always," said Foxfield suddenly.

"I've heard of that idea you're alluding to, Mr Foxfield," said the old gentleman. "You mean that idea about the chromosomes."

"Now tell me," said the barrister, relapsing for a moment. "I've heard somewhere before of this idea you're speaking of. I'm told these cosmic rays affect, what is it you call them?—mutations."

"I have no doubt of it," said Foxfield.

"You'll find no physicist to encourage you," said the old gentleman.

"Or contradict me," said Foxfield.

"Aye, ay," said the old gentleman cheerfully. "It's a case of not proven."

"But what is this?" asked Davis. "Do you mean that these—these cosmic rays may affect heredity—inheritance?"

"I should be inclined to say they must," said Foxfield.

"But why them in particular?" asked the barrister.

60

"Because we have eliminated almost every other possible cause for changes in the chromosomes."

"It's a most extraordinary thing," said the rufous man, slowly waking up and passing by swift stages from sleepiness to bright alertness.

"The chromosomes," said Foxfield, "the germinal elements, have very complicated and enormous molecules. They are rather elaborately protected from most types of disturbance. They have a sort of independence of the parent body. They go their way alone."

"Transmission of acquired characteristics strictly forbidden,"[28] someone interjected.

"It seems to be. But the X rays, the Gamma rays, and particularly these cosmic rays *can* get through, and so, I reason, they must get through—to start something fresh. Since something fresh is always being started."

And now it was Foxfield's turn to answer intelligent questions and give a brief lecture.

He summarized the new realizations of the past twenty-five years about mutations and survival almost as expertly as the old professor had elucidated his atoms. He showed how the changing of species bit by bit, by imperceptible gradations, which the early Darwinians had stressed, had given place in modern evolutionary theory to a realization of the frequency of extensive simultaneous sports and mutations. And there was nothing in the circumstances of an animal species which could explain these sports and mutations. And so it was that Foxfield was compelled to think they were produced by some penetrating exterior force.

"But why not Providence?" asked the quiet man.

"Because the vast majority of these mutations are aimless and useless," said Foxfield.

"And so, having eliminated everything else," said the barrister, "you lay the burden of change and mutation—and in fact all the responsibility for evolution—on those little cosmic rays! Countless myriads fly by and miss. Then one hits—Ping! Ping!—and we get a double-headed calf or a superman."

"What an *unsettled* universe it is!" said someone.

3

And then suddenly the rufous man was touched by fantasy. His sleepiness had fallen from him altogether. He sat up brightly now. "Look here!" he said. "I've got an idea! Suppose—"

He paused. He produced that "suppose" like a juicy fruit and hovered with his hand in the air for a voluptuous moment before he squeezed the juice from it.

"Suppose these cosmic rays come from Mars!"

"They come, I tell ye, from every direction," said the old professor.

"Including Mars. Yes, Mars, that wizened elder brother of the planet Earth. Mars, where intelligent life has gone on far beyond anything this planet has ever known. Mars, the planet which is being frozen out, exhausted, done for. Some of you may have read a book called The War of the Worlds—I forget who wrote it—Jules Verne, Conan Doyle, one of those fellows. But it told how the Martians invaded the world, wanted to colonize it, and exterminate mankind. Hopeless attempt! They couldn't stand the different atmospheric pressure, they couldn't stand the difference in gravitation; bacteria finished them up. Hopeless from the start. The only impossible thing in the story was to imagine that the Martians would be fools enough to try anything of the sort. But—"

He held up his hand and waggled his fingers with pleasure at his idea.

"Suppose they say up there: 'Let's start varying and modifying life on earth. Let's change it. Let's get at the human character and the human brain and make it Martian-minded. Let's stop having children on this rusty little old planet of ours, and let's change men until they become in effect our children. Let's get spiritual children there.' D'you see? Martian minds in seasoned terrestrial bodies."

"And so they start firing away at us with these cosmic rays!"

"And presently," said the rufous man, almost gobbling with the excitement of his idea, "presently when they have got the world Martianized—"

"I never heard such nonsense," said the old professor and got up to go away. "I tell ye these cosmic rays come from every direction."

"And why shouldn't they use a sort of shrapnel?" said the rufous man to his retreating back. "Shells full of these cosmic rays, so to speak, with a back-lash. Nothing impossible in that, is there?"

The old professor's back made no reply. And yet it had a certain eloquence.

"They'd probably begin with wild mutations," somebody suggested after a pause; "and then get more accurate."

"It may have been going on for a long time," said the quiet man, helpful as ever.

"You're assuming of course that they know a lot more about us than we know about them," said the rising barrister.

"And isn't that easily possible?" the rufous man countered. "Mars is the older planet. Far beyond us along the line of evolution. What we know is nothing to what *they* must know. They may be as able to look through us as we are to take a microscope and look through an amoeba. And when they have got the world Martianized, when they've started a race here with minds like their own and yet with bodies fit for earth, when they have practically interbred with us and ousted our strain, *then* they'll begin to send along their treasures, their apparatus—*grafting* their life on ours. Making men into their heirs and their continuation. Eh? Am I talking nonsense, Foxfield? Am I talking nonsense?"

"The jokes of today may become the facts of tomorrow," said Foxfield. "Nonsense *pro tem* let us say."

"I'm beginning to believe my own story," said the rufous man. "With your endorsement. It's wonderful."

"But tell me," said the lawyer also a little excited by this strange idea, "is there any evidence in confirmation? Any evidence at all? For example—has there been any increase of freaks and monsters in the world in the last few years?"

"It's only recently that there has been any attempt to give a statistical account of abnormalities and mutations," said Foxfield. "Monstrosities are hushed up—human monstrosities particularly. Even animal-breeders have a sort of shame about them, and wild creatures kill strange offspring instinctively. Every living creature seems to want to breed *true*. But from the fruit-fly and plants and so on we know there is an amount of variation going on—much larger than everyday people imagine."

"Mostly unfavourable variation though?" asked the barrister.

"Nine hundred and ninety-nine per cent," said Foxfield. "With no survival value at all. Chance. Like the wildest experimenting. . . ."

4

Now this was the last kind of stuff to which an anxious prospective parent on the verge of neurasthenia ought to have listened.

And yet is it not out of accidents and disasters and fantastic twists of the mind that the greatest discoveries of science and the profoundest revelation of Nature's processes have come? Things long unsuspected may be laid bare by a jest. The jokes of today may become the facts of tomorrow, even as Foxfield had said.

As Mr Joseph Davis walked home from the Planetarium Club he seemed to hear and see those cosmic rays, flashing like tracer bullets, singing like arrows, gleaming and vanishing like falling stars, through the world about him. You might wrap yourself from them, the old professor had remarked, in solid lead, and still they got through to you.

CHAPTER 3

Mr Joseph Davis Wrestles with an Incredible Idea

1

It is an open question how freely an obstetrician should talk to the husband of his patient. Dr Holdman Stedding erred perhaps on the communicative side. It may be he should have realized more promptly that Mr Joseph Davis was troubled in his imagination, and he should have exercised more care than he did in avoiding topics that might intensify his imaginative disturbance. Yet it may be pleaded in extenuation that it was Mr Davis who started the subject of these mysterious extra-terrestrial radiations and that it was Dr Holdman Stedding who was taken by surprise with a novel idea. He too had his imaginative side. He liked novel ideas and there was just that streak of scientific curiosity and communicativeness in him which impairs discretion.

He was a stout, large-faced, warmish-blond man, always a little out of breath and always with a faint flavour of surprise in his expression. And he liked to be made to laugh. His mouth was always just a little open, as if ready to laugh. But he knew his work marvelously well; he had strong and skilful hands and he never got flurried.

Davis had called on him before. He had wanted to have an exact account of the health of his wife. Was she strong enough to bear a child? She was as strong, said Dr Holdman Stedding, "As a young pony."

The way in which Davis beat about that idea that things were not quite right with his wife gave the good doctor a queer feeling that a less reassuring reply would have been more acceptable. For obscure reasons—sub-reasons rather—it seemed that Davis did not want this child.

Like every practicing obstetrician Dr Holdman Stedding knew all the faint intimations of a tentative to abortion, and knew how to nip any such suggestion in the bud. Panic before fatherhood is a more frequent thing than the lay mind realizes. It is constantly peeping out in these consultations. Davis, if such had been his disposition, had departed unsatisfied. But here he was again.

"I suppose everything is going all right with Mary?" he asked, advancing uneasily into the consulting-room.

"Couldn't be better."

"You made a second examination?"

"At your request. It was unnecessary."

"There is nothing unusual . . . ?" Mr Davis rephrased his question. "The child, the embryo, so far as you can ascertain, is not different in any way from any other child at the same stage?"

"It is coming on well. There is absolutely no ground for worry."

"And the mother—physically and mentally. You are sure she can stand this? Because, you know, say what you like, she is not a normal woman."

"Do sit down," said the doctor, recapturing the hearth-rug by putting his visitor into a chair, and then standing over him. "Don't you think, Mr Davis, that you are—just a trifle *fanciful* about your wife?"

"Well," said Davis, sticking to his point, "*is* she normal?"

"Few women in her condition remain as sane and healthy as she is. If that is abnormal. Her mind like her body is as sound as a bell."

"You don't think a woman can be too sane? I confess, Dr Stedding, I don't always understand my wife. There is a sort of hard scepticism in her mind. . . . You don't think a woman can be *too* intelligent to make a good mother?"

"Really, Mr Davis! What's fretting your mind? With her clearheadedness and your literary genius your child may be something quite outstanding."

"And that is what bothers me. The fact of it is, Doctor, I've been hearing talk lately. . . . I don't know if you know Foxfield and his work. . . . I take a scientific interest in this as well as a personal one. . . . The point is—"

2

He kept the doctor waiting for a moment.

"The point is; do you, with your experience, think that latterly—how shall I put it?—exceptional children have become rather more *frequent* than they used to be?"

"Exceptional? Gifted?"

"Yes, gifted. In some cases perhaps. And also what shall I say?—abnormalities?"

"H'm!" said the doctor. He was interested. He attempted a brief survey of his experience. "There *are* some rather surprising children and youngsters about. But I suppose something of that sort has always been going on."

"To the same extent?" pressed Davis. "To the same extent?"

"Possibly not. It is very hard to say. Naturally in this part of London and with a clientele like mine, we have exceptional parents. My impression, my unchecked and uncontrolled impression, is that, in the world I know, maternal mortality is extremely low and the infants are—*bright* is the word. Some with biggish heads. But anything in the way of out-of-the-way novelties, no. If you are worrying about monstrosities—you need not worry. And exceptionally bright children are nothing to worry about. The Caesarean operation is probably more frequent nowadays. . . . That may be due rather to improved gynaecology than to any increase in mutations. . . ."

Pause.

"I would like to talk to you rather fantastically," said Davis abruptly. "It's not only my wife I am thinking about. Don't think I'm mad in what I am saying to you, but just think I am letting my imagination out for a romp."

"Nothing better," said Dr Holdman Stedding, who like most medical practitioners nowadays had a disposition towards a rather amateurish psycho-analysis. "Say what you like. Let it rip."

"Well," said Mr Davis, and hesitated at the strangeness and difficulty of the ideas he had to explain. "Biologists—I was talking to Foxfield the other day—biologists say that when a species comes to a difficult phase in its struggle for existence—and I suppose no one can say that is not fairly true of the human situation nowadays—there is an increased disposition to vary. There is—how did Foxfield put it?—for one thing there is less insistence on the normal. Less insistence on the normal. It is as if the species began to try round and feel for new possibilities."

"Ye-es." Said the doctor, with non-committal encouragement in his tone.

"And as if it became more capable of accepting abnormalities and weaving them into its destinies."

"Yes," said the doctor, weighing the proposition. "That is in accordance with current ideas."

"As an industrious student of history," began Mr Davis. "You know I have written one or two books?"

"Who does not? My two nephews got your *Alexander, or Youth the Conqueror* and your *Story of the Spanish Main* as prizes last term, and I can assure you I read them myself with great delight."

"Well. It seems to me that for ages human life has been playing much the same tune with variations—but much the same tune. What we call human nature. The general behaviour, the normal system of reactions, has been the same. The old old story. Abnormal people have been kept in their places. You don't think, doctor, that that uniformity of human experience is going to be disturbed?"

"I wish you would explain a little more."

"Suppose there are—*Martians.*"

"Well?"

"Suppose there are beings, real material beings like ourselves, in another planet, but far wiser, more intelligent, much more highly developed. Suppose they are able to see us and know about us—as we know about the creatures under a microscope, which have no suspicion of us.[29] . . . Mind you, this isn't my idea. I'm only repeating something I heard in the club. But suppose that in some way these older, wiser, greater, and better organized intelligences are able to influence human life."

"How?"

"They may have tried all sorts of ways. They may have been experimenting for ages. Much as we might run a reagent into a microscope slide. The amoebae and so on would have no idea. . . ."

68

"If you are thinking of anything like interplanetary telepathy, anything of that sort, I'm not with you. Even between closely similar minds, between identical twins for example, I doubt if such a thing is possible. . . . I *detest* telepathy."

"This is quite a different idea."

"Well?"

"Suppose that for the last few thousand years they have been experimenting in human genetics. Suppose they have been trying to alter mankind in some way, through the human genes."

"But how?"

"You have heard of cosmic rays, Doctor?"

The doctor took it in with some deliberation. "It is a *quite* fantastic idea," he said after a pause.

"But neither impossible nor incredible."

"Some things one puts outside the range of practical possibility."

"And some things refuse to be put outside the range of practical possibility."

"But you don't mean to tell me you believe—?"

"No. But I face a possibility with an open mind."

"Which is?"

"That these Martians—"

"But we don't know there *are* any Martians!"

"We don't know that there aren't."

"No."

"Quite possibly these rays do not come from Mars—more probably than not. But—let us call the senders—"

"*Senders?*"

"Well, whatever originates them. Let us call them Martians—just to avoid inventing a new name—"

"Very well. And your suggestion is—?"

"That these Martians have been firing away with increasing accuracy and effectiveness at our chromosomes—perhaps for long ages. That is the story, the fancy, if you like, that I want in some way to put to the test. Every now and then in history, strange exceptional figures have appeared, Confucius, Buddha; men with strange memories, men with uncanny mathematical gifts, men with unaccountable intuitions.

69

Mostly they have been persons in advance of their times, as we say, and out of step with their times. . . . Do you see what I am driving at, doctor?"

"But this is the purest fantasy!"

"Or the realization of a fantastic fact."

"But—!"

3

Dr Holdman Stedding wavered in his mind. Ought he to let this talk run on or close down on it forthwith?

At least half the disordered minds of the present time, he reflected, develop delusions about radiations. That kind of fancy has largely replaced those spiritual visions and inner voices which supplied the demented with crazy interpretations of their perplexities in the past. It was *dangerous* stuff, and the mind of Davis, to say the least of it, was very delicately poised. And yet there was something faintly plausible—a sort of fairy-tale plausibility—about this idea that caught the unprofessional elements of the doctor's imagination. He went on taking the idea seriously.

"What sort of confirmation *is* possible?" he considered.

"That is where the puzzle comes in. That is why I am consulting you."

"You think that if one attempted some sort of examination of human births, past and present—it would of course be very hard to get any adequate records about this sort of thing—one might be able to detect—?"

"That we are being played upon."

"But you don't *believe*—?"

"Not a bit of it. Oh, no! I didn't come here to be certified. I am advancing a certain hypothesis. I am being purely scientific in my method. I advance a provisional theory that a certain thing is going on. And, mind you, if anything of the sort *is* going on, it is of great—of supreme importance to our race. And having made our trial assumption, we try and work out what would be some of the logical consequences of this process of extra-terrestrial influence, if my theory proves to hold good. Is it possible to detect non-human characteristics, superhuman characteristics perhaps, in some of the children born nowadays, and are these non-human characteristics on the increase? Are there people—what shall I call them?—*fey* people about? People as sane as you and I and yet strange? We can try them with special intelligence tests perhaps. We can go into the reports of educational institutions. So far I have not planned the lay-out of this investigation. It is all quite new in my mind. But isn't it a legitimate inquiry? I ask you."

"You will need genius for that lay-out."

"Every original research needs that. But my theory I think is plain. My theory is that new influences are being brought to bear on human reproduction. For the purposes of our research I call the source of these influences—*Martians*. If my suspicions are confirmed, these Martians for purposes at which we can only guess—are thrusting mutations upon us. They are experimenting with human mutations. They are planning human mutations. So that presently our very children may not prove to be our own!"

As Mr Davis said these last words, a full realization of the indiscretion of this talk dawned upon Dr Holdman Stedding.

"But that is going too far!" he cried. "That is going much too far. We are talking—we are amusing ourselves—with pseudo-scientific non-sense."

Mr Davis perceived quite clearly what was in his interlocutor's mind. "It is too late, doctor, to say that to me. This notion has bitten me. I mean to devote myself to this investigation; I feel called to it; and I want you to interest yourself in it also. If there is one chance in a million of this suspicion being true, then it demands attention. Even on the chance so bare as that we ought to get watchers and searchers, planetary coast-guards, so to speak, at work. We have to specify and measure and determine the nature of this inflow and herd it back upon itself before it is too late."

"H'm," said Doctor Holdman Stedding, regarding his queer visitor with an expression of infinite perplexity.

"I am under no delusions," said Mr Davis. "I agree I am talking about something almost absolutely improbable. Let me make it clear to you that I am perfectly clear upon that. I am skirting the giddy edge of utter impossibility. Well and good. But sometimes there are intuitions.

How many discoveries have flashed forth at first as the wildest of surmises? It may be circumstances have conspired to point my mind in a certain direction. Never mind about that. I myself do not feel that this is an impossibility. Just simply that—not an absolute impossibility. No more. That is where I stand."

CHAPTER 4

Dr Holdman Stedding is Infected with the Idea

1

Dr Holdman Stedding lay awake that night thinking about the state of mind of Mr Davis and about the queer idea of a genetic invasion of Martian qualities that he had propounded. There was something provocative about the idea; something that made his intelligence bristle defensively. "Pure balderdash!" he said aloud, but as a matter of fact what made it so irritating was that it was not pure balderdash. There was an attenuated but unbreakable thread of silly plausibility about the suggestion that prevented him from throwing it altogether out of his mind. He threw words like "balderdash" at it as one might throw stones at a dog that persists in following one, and presently there was the damned thing back again.

"If it *should* chance that something of the sort was going on. . . ."

He found himself asking himself whether there was any sort of evidence that some new type or perhaps even new types of human being were appearing in the world. Can there be such things as Martianized minds? "Silly phrase," he said. "But somehow a contagious phrase."

He ran his mind over its collection of facts about the subject. He knew most of what was known and he realized that for the purpose of getting a conclusive answer, it amounted to hardly anything at all. He reviewed the question methodically. The most confident statements, he reflected, are made that man has not changed since Neolithic times, that he has degenerated since the days of Pericles, that he is larger or smaller, healthier, less healthy than his ancestors, that he has become finer and subtler or anything else that suits the private convictions stated or implicit, of the "authority" who flings out this sort of stuff to the public. When you come to think it over as he was doing it was all without exception opinionated rubbish. No one has yet devised the means of getting the confused and irregular records available into any sort of order. No one has been able to do that work. People like J. B. S. Haldane[30] and suchlike pioneer biologists were trying to form a research society now. Even the men most in contact with the facts have nothing better than "impressions" and "persuasions," and some, thought Dr Holdman Stedding with righteous self-applause, know that that is so, and some do not and let their prejudices rip. Dr Holdman Stedding's private and unproven "impression" was just the impression most favourable to Mr Davis's wild surmise. His unproven belief was that a considerable change in the human mind was going on. He thought that heavy and clumsy types were not so abundant in the population as they used to be and that certain new mental types were on the increase.

"But what has that to do with Martians and cosmic rays?" his common sense protested, and his common sense answered "Nothing."

After which he continued to pursue the subject.

2

Such discursive nocturnal meditations as Dr Holdman Stedding was now committed to, combine the advantage that they cover a wide ground and find the most diverse evidence in their excursions, with the disadvantage that they sometimes lose their way altogether and never return to the main issue. For a time the doctor's train of thought was in danger of the latter fate. He wandered into a labyrinth of possibility about the peculiar scepticism of the contemporary mind and the perplexing obduracies and wilfulnesses of so many of the rising generation. He knew more about the ideas of his hospital students than most of his colleagues, and sometimes they filled him with hope and sometimes they terrified him. Like all youth since our race began, most of them were sheep and went whither they were told or led, but for all that it was quite conceivable that the proportion of independent and wilful minds was higher than it had ever been before.

The stiff troublesome fellows were the interesting ones.

He passed to the marked increase of effective medical research and from that to the general inventiveness of our age. Inventiveness had never been so manifest as it was today. For more than a century it had been increasing. Directly you said a thing could not possibly be done, there it was—done. Yet so far no one had suggested that this must be due to the release of new mental types. It might be.

He felt that he would like to have another talk with Davis about the whole matter. Where had Davis got his evidently very strong belief that there were new and strange types appearing in the world? Could he know of anything that a leading obstetrician of wide scientific reading was not likely to know? The trouble about talking to Davis was the doctor's persuasion—possibly an exaggerated one—that mentally he was not too safely balanced. It would be unwise to "encourage" him, if he was in fact drifting towards a delusion. And then abruptly Dr Holdman Stedding remembered something.

"His wife!"

Several times Davis had practically asserted that his wife was strange, odd, exceptional. Dr Holdman Stedding tried to recall the exact words but he found that he could not do so. But that manifest disturbance at the advent of a child was bound up with that.

"If he's beginning to think his wife is one of these Martianized people! . . . I wonder what a fellow of that sort might not do. . . . What was it he said? Something about our very children not proving to be our own?"

Dr Holdman Stedding spent some time that night trying to recall every particular he could of both these people. She was very quiet in her manner, observant, sane. If she was exceptional mentally it was because she was exceptionally sane. She moved easily and gracefully, as one does who has no conflicting nervous impulses. She did so even in her present condition; she was being one of the calmest and most competent patients he had ever known. "If she's Martianized," reflected the doctor, "then the sooner we all get Martianized the better."

But then, he considered, he had not seen her a dozen times altogether and there might be qualities in her of which he knew nothing, to account for her husband's attitude, for that faintly distrustful insecurity about her.

The doctor speculated about the relations of the Davis couple for a while. He liked her and he found something slightly antipathetic about her husband. The man's quick, incalculable and ill-adjusted mental movements made him uncomfortable. No doubt his literary gifts were considerable, but like so many of these literary people he had much more control over himself upon paper than in real life. He must be a great trial to her and she ought to be protected, now at any rate, from his possible eccentricities. The doctor felt that something ought to be done about it, and began thinking of possible things that might or might not be done, until it occurred to him that it was through this sort of breach in impartiality that unprofessional conduct may enter into the life of a practitioner.

3

In the morning he wrote a very carefully considered letter to Davis which he marked "Private" and addressed to the Planetarium Club.

It was a long and repetitious letter. It beat about the bush too much to be quoted in full here, but the gist of it was a warning not to give way to a "fantasy-suggestion." "These little imaginative ideas one takes into one's mind are like those insidious creatures the mediaeval doctors used to talk about, little things that seem nothing at all, that leap into your mouth before you know where you are and grow into monsters inside your brain and devour your sanity." No human mind, the doctor declared, was sufficiently balanced as yet to resist the disturbance of a too persistently cherished idea. That was why nearly everyone who investigated "psychic phenomena" or "telepathy" or "astrology" or "cheiromancy" or the tarot cars presently began to find there was "something in it." Mr Davis was to think no more about it, distract his mind, take up chess, play golf on new courses, before this obsession really gripped his mind. "You are standing on the brink of a long mental slide at the bottom of which is delusional insanity. I write plainly to you, because you are still a perfectly sane man."

4

"He knows—he knows as well as I do," said Mr Joseph Davis. "But he's afraid to go on with it. . . .

"I *want* to go on with it. But how I am to do that I don't know. Watch. . . . And meanwhile these cosmic rays fly noiselessly about me—the arrows of the Martians—and by a birth here and a birth there—humanity undergoes—dehumanization."

CHAPTER 5

Professor Ernest Keppel takes up the Idea in His Own Peculiar Fashion

1

Now Doctor Holdman Stedding had a great friend and crony, a bachelor like himself and a queer imaginative talker, Professor Ernest Keppel. He was nominally professor of philosophy, but latterly he had engaged more and more in psychotherapy. He was accused of psychologizing his philosophy away into a descriptive science and he was a frequent and formidable controversialist, more often in hot water than not.

He was a dark, scarred, halting man. He had been scarred by the explosion of a hidden mine in the German trenches during the September advance in 1918. The scar ran as a dark red suture from the middle of his forehead across the left brow, where an overhanging exostosis thrust his eye into a deep and sinister cavern. Moreover the explosion had stiffened the joint of his forearm, injured his pelvis, and left him lame. Before that he must have been very animated and attractive indeed. But his mutilation had left a curious bitterness in his nature. He understood why he was bitter; he did his best not to be bitter but taking thought about it could not make him sweet. He was over-sensitive to the effect of his scar when he met new people; his incurable delusion that he was repulsive made him abrupt and rude, more particularly with women, and perhaps he exaggerated the delights of the normal experiences from which he felt he was shut off. He was prosperous and he lived well, and his energy and persistence in research and speculation were making a great reputation for him.

The doctor found his company extremely stimulating. He was accustomed to bring new ideas to him and toast them, so to speak, in front of his glowing mind. Indeed he hardly ever took an idea to himself and assimilated it until he had warmed it up first before Professor Keppel. And now accordingly he took advantage of a lunch engagement to bring up the matter of the Martians. They often arranged by telephone to lunch together, because Keppel's place was so much nearer than clubland.

"I was talking to a lunatic yesterday," said the doctor, "and he broached a most remarkable idea."

He sketched Mr Davis's alleged discovery in a tone of appreciative scepticism as lunch went on.

"It's nonsense," he concluded.

"It's nonsense," Professor Keppel agreed. "But—"

"Exactly! But—"

"But—" repeated Keppel and waved the hand of his inferior arm stiffly, while his trim parlourmaid stood at his elbow with the savoury.

A certain brightness appeared in his overhung eye. His expression became profound.

Dr Holdman Stedding waited.

"The interesting point," said Professor Keppel, helping himself to his *Gruyere à la Roi Alphonse*, "The interesting point is, as you say, that we do in fact know nothing about what human modification may be going on at the present time. Nothing. Demographic science has hardly begun to be a precise science—much less an exact science. Our social statistics are extravagantly clumsy. (A) We don't know what to count or measure and (B) we haven't an idea how to measure it. It is quite possible that new human types may be appearing in the world, or that once rare types may be increasing in number relatively. More geniuses—more aberrant gifts. And the queer thing is that when this lunatic comes to you and starts this idea in your head, you don't say Pish or Tush and just turn it down; you being to have a vague sense that somehow you have felt something—you hardly know what."

"That's it."

"And when you bring it to me (Do try this savoury. Don't pass it. I got the recipe from Martinez at that Spanish restaurant in Swallow Street) I begin to have the same feeling."

2

"One's imagination wants to play with it. It's as attractive as a hare's foot to a kitten. Suppose Keppel, suppose—for the sake of a talk—there *are* Martians.

"Let's suppose it. I'm more than willing."

"What sort of minds would they have and what would they think of our minds and what might they not try to make of them?"

"Regarded as an exercise in speculative general psychology? That's attractive."

"As a speculative exercise then."

"Exactly. You know that man Olaf Stapledon has already tried something of the sort in a book called *Last and First Men*.[31] Some day we shall certainly have to come to a general psychology independent of the human type, just as now these young men in the Society of Experimental Biology are getting away from the highly specialized peculiarities of human physiology towards a general physiological science. Now away there in Mars, as any astronomer will tell you, there are all the conditions necessary for a sort of life similar, if not identically similar, to life upon earth, the same elements, air, water, a temperature range not widely different. The probabilities are in favour of there having been a parallel—a roughly parallel evolution. Parallel but in some ways different. The gravitational energy, atmospheric pressure and suchlike things are different and that would mean differences in lightness, vigour and size. Martian plants and animals would probably run much bigger. *Much* bigger."

"I forget the relative masses of the two planets," said the doctor.

"I forget too. Roughly it's something like eight to one—perhaps a bit more. So the Martian if he had a human form would be twice as tall and eight times our weight. A bigger, longer-lived creature. Assuming—"

"What *don't* we assume!"

"No. It's not *wild* assumption. The odds are in favour that there are or have been growths, detachments, moving feeling things, in existence on that planet. This is bold speculation, Holdman Stedding, I admit, but it isn't extravaganza."

"Go on. But you wouldn't dare to talk to your students like this."

"Possibly not. How far would the evolution of life, if it had an independent start elsewhere under slightly but not essentially different conditions, run parallel to the evolution of life on earth?"

"The same tune, I suppose, with variations."

"It is difficult to imagine anything else. There would be plants—I think green plants—and animals. The animals would run about as individuals and have senses, something like ours—perhaps very like ours. They might see more colours than we do, for example, have a longer or shorter range of sound, subtler feelers in the place of our hands. Probably Nature has tried out all the possible senses on earth here. But not all the possible shapes and patterns. Anyhow these Martians would respond to stimuli; they would have reflexes; they would condition their reflexes. I believe if we could call up the spirit of dear old Pavlov,[32] we should find him agreeing with us, that the chances are heavily in favour of any possible minds there, being minds fundamentally like ours."

"But with a longer past."

"Yes, Mars was cool long before earth was. A longer past, a hotter summer and a harder winter—the year of Mars is twice the length of ours—a larger body and a larger brain. With more room for memories—more and better memories, and more space for ideas, more and better ideas. And so the problem comes down to this. What sort of mind would a man have if he had a longer ancestry, an ampler memory, a less hurried life?"

"I accept all that as just possible," said the doctor.

"It is certainly where the weight of probability lies. Now all these pseudo-scientific story writers who write about Mars make their Martians monsters and horrors, inhuman in the bad sense, cruel. Why should they be anything of the sort? Why," repeated Professor Keppel, taking coffee, "why should they be anything of the sort?"[33]

"Quite nice monsters?"

"Why not?"

"Well, the German professor evolved his idea of a camel from his inner consciousness; why shouldn't we do the same with our Martians?"

"Having regard to the facts. Why not?"

Dr Holdman Stedding looked at his watch.

"Not till you've smoked one of those pennant-shaped Coronas you like," said Keppel, "and just a whiff of brandy. Because, confound it! you started this talk, you've interested me, and you've got to hear it out. If there is such a thing as a Martian, rest assured, Holdman Stedding, he's humanity's big brother."

"Big in every way you think. A super-superman."

"Good anyhow."

"Beyond good and evil?"[34]

"Everything alive must have its good and evil. Beyond *our* good and evil anyhow. None the worse for that perhaps. No; if you talk to your lunatic again you can at least dispel any fear he has of his Martians. The odds are they are not so much invading us as acting as a sort of interplanetary tutor. Bless my heart! At the mere thought I feel a sort of benevolent influence."

"No," said Mr Holdman Stedding, emitting a smoke jet with the appreciative expression of a cigar advertisement in *Punch*[35] and weighing the possibilities of the case with luxurious deliberation. "It's your cook."

3

"She's a very good cook," Professor Keppel admitted. "But about these Martians. We are letting our fancy play too wildly about them. Let's leave them for a bit. There's another point your patient has raised that's quite available for separate treatment. Practically another question. There may or may not be these sane and mature watchers over human destiny, these Celestial Uncles, these friends in the midnight sky, but what does seem to be possible and even within our reach, is this idea, that the species *Homo sapiens*, because of some possible increase or change in direction of the cosmic rays, or from some unknown cause, is starting to mutate, and mutate along some such line as that larger wisdom indicates."

"Some *sort* of larger wisdom," said Dr Holdman Stedding, "a purely hypothetical wisdom."

"You are very precise," said Professor Keppel. "But anyhow that is what we want to know. Is there such a biological movement going on? Is there any means of tracing it if it is going on? The real feeling at the back of both our minds is that if there is not something of the sort going on, then this breed of pretentious, self-protective imbeciles—"

"Poor *Homo sapiens!*" murmured the doctor. "How he catches it nowadays!"

"It is very near the end of its tether.[36] It's no good pretending you disagree with that. Haven't all reasonable civilized men nowadays this feeling of being dilettantes on a sinking ship? We all want a break towards something better in the way of living. Hopes and our wishes speak together. And it may be—as we half hope. But how are we to test this idea? How are we to set about the investigation?"

"Without making everyone think we have gone crazy?"

"Precisely."

"Nietzsche?" hazarded the doctor. "Are these his supermen we are thinking about?"

"He brings in too much oriental bric-à-brac for my taste," said Keppel. "And so far as I can make out, he has at least two different meanings for that Übermensch of his. On the one hand is a biologically better sort of man and on the other a sort of aggregate synthetic being like Hobbes's *Leviathan.*[37] You never know how to take him. Let's rule Nietzsche out. Let us just follow up this question whether there is an increase in—what shall I call them?—high-grade intellectual types."

The doctor helped himself with infinite restraint and discretion to just the merest splash more brandy. "I think Keppel, there may be a possible way to set this note of interrogation working."

"We have our reputations to consider."

"We have our reputations to consider, but quite possibly this fellow —well, to commit a very slight indiscretion—it is Mr Joseph Davis, the man who writes those extremely popular, those *florid*—shall I say?— those almost too glorifying *glosses*, so to speak, on history—might do something for us in this respect. His writings, his association with what one might call the more romantic aspects of the human record, his almost strained belief in the faith, hope and glory of our species, put him, I think, in a position to ask questions. . . ."

"Joseph Davis," considered Keppel. "The man who wrote *From Agincourt to Trafalgar?*[38] Him. You got this idea about the Martians from him!"

"I told him to think no more about it."

"But he will?"

"He will. He wants to think about it. He wants to follow this up. He—Something has shaken him up. I can't make up my mind whether he is going mad or going sane. But if I give him half a hint, he'll be off on the scent of these Martians now like a dog after a rabbit."

CHAPTER 6

Opening Phases of the
Great Eugenic Research

1

"Now here, now there," whispered Mr Davis to himself as he stood on the doorstep of the headmaster of Gorpel School and looked at the headmaster's trim but beautiful garden.

It was six months later and high summer and he was the father of an extremely healthy but extremely intelligent-looking child. And the belief that he had discovered that the most wonderful event in the history of our planet was now happening, had entered into and become part of his being.

Ostensibly he had come to Gorpel to lecture on "The Grandeur That Was Rome," but really he had come to look that interesting collection of boys over and talk to the headmaster about any mentally (or even physically) exceptional lads who might have attracted his attention. Nothing was to be said about Martians, cosmic rays or anything of that sort. It was to be put before the headmaster as a mild little enquiry into the prospects of the "odd" type of boy.[39]

It was Dr Holdman Stedding who had suggested this line of enquiry to him. Really the excellent doctor wanted this material collected to feed the whimsical and nine-tenths sceptical curiosity of Keppel and himself, but he had succeeded in persuading himself that it was absolutely the best treatment for Davis's mental worries that his imaginative vagaries should be steadied and assuaged by a methodical exploration of what might quite possibly prove to be illuminating facts. This brought with it a certain sense of benevolence, because Davis was not his patient under treatment, paid no fees. It was indeed simply helping the man as one man helps another.

Davis at this stage was looking for mental abnormalities—on the upward side. He was getting whatever could be got from prison governors, educational authorities, schools of every sort where there was close contact between teachers and pupils, even from army instructors, institutions for defectives, lunatic asylums—and making a general report and a digest of his results. A number of facts not generally known was emerging from these enquiries. The proportion of children of the calculating-boy and musical-prodigy type seemed to be increasing quite markedly; finer muscular adjustment was in a very conspicuous way ousting mere beef from athleticism; critical obduracy at quite an early age was far more in evidence than it had ever been before.

Possibly Davis, like many investigators, was disposed to find what he looked for. Dr Holdman Stedding fancied he could allow for that.

What Dr Holdman Stedding did not allow for were the practical effects of these preoccupations upon an author's normal activities. Like most men of sound professional standing he thought authors did their work outside time and space and occupied their normal hours in the pursuit of royalties and publicity and in making speeches on irrelevant topics to unnecessary societies. But Joseph Davis had been engaged upon a great constellation of books, which were to give history, ennobled and illuminated, to the common man. He had schemed that as what he called his "life task." That task was now beginning to look like a modern cathedral under construction when some new heresy breaks out among the more opulent faithful and funds run short. Sometimes for six or seven days not a line was added.

Meanwhile every day it grew plainer to Davis that this theory, which had at first seemed even to him a fantastic hypothesis, was real and true. A new quality of human being was being inserted into the fabric of human life, "one here, one there."

It was hard not to talk about it. It was hard to have to keep up the pretence of making a mere respectable enquiry as trivial and pointless as—let us say—a research thesis in pedagogics for an American University. He went about the world to social gatherings, to assemblies and theatres and restaurants; he mingled in crowds, he watched people's unsuspecting faces, and now the thought was always in his mind: *If only they knew!*

If only they knew what the Martians were doing to them!

At first his attitude had been one of stark antagonism to this Martian intrusion. He had something more than an ordinary man's instinctive loyalty to race and kind. He had super-imposed a mental habit. He had made himself a champion of that ancient and venerable normal life of humanity, unaltered through the ages—except now and then through the providential punishment of some transitory heresy— the simple, old, beautiful story of childhood, learning, love, industry, parentage, honour, and the easy passage to a venerable old age and a brightly hopeful death. It was a story at once earthly, in the best, the honest pious peasant sense, and profoundly spiritual. This life, age after age, had been set in a stimulating round of seedtime and harvest, cold and heat, thirst and hunger, reasonable desires and modest satisfactions. Of such stuff was history woven, and across this sound, enduring fabric were embroidered the great historical figures, in a bright opera-drama as glad in quality as an illuminated missal. History told of their conquests, triumphs, glories, heroisms, of heart-stirring tragedies and lovely sacrifices. They were all far greater than life-size—like the monarchs and gods in an Assyrian relief—the common people ran about beneath their feet according to the best historical traditions. So it had been. So it would go on until at last the Almighty commanded the curtain to ring down and called the actors forward from their various retiring-rooms, to receive appropriate rewards.

Such was the picture of the world and its promise that he had been working to realize, overworking to realize, when this fantastic and distracting suspicion of a Martian intervention first came to him. It was as if the vast canvas on which he had been working with such resolution had suddenly cracked across and betrayed his light and shade, his heights and depths, as the completest unreality.

Now—and here there seems to have been some gap in his logical process—he felt that the Martians would certainly be against all these fine things for which he struggled. Why, one may ask, should the Martians be against them? Why should they be by necessity spoilers of so rich and noble a fabric? But he had his full share of that infirmity of our impatient minds[40] which makes us leap naturally to the conclusion that what is not uncritically on our side and subject to our ideas, is against us. At the onset of a strange way of living we bristle like dogs at the sight of a strange animal. He hated these Martians as soon as he thought of them. He could not imagine their interference with our nice world could be anything but devastating.

His motive to begin with, therefore, was an altogether uncomplicated desire to detect, expose and repel an insidious and dreadful attack upon this dear and happy human life we all enjoy so greatly and relinquish so reluctantly. These Martians presented themselves to him as the blackest of threats to all those convictions that make life worth living upon earth. Indisputably they must be inhuman, whatever else they are. That went without saying. To be inhuman implied to him, as to most of us, malignant cruelty; it seemed impossible that it could mean anything else (And yet this is a world where lots of us live upon terms of sentimental indulgence towards cats, dogs, monkeys, horses, cows and suchlike unhuman creatures, help them in a myriad simple troubles and attribute the most charming reactions to them!)

Among other things it seemed to him unquestionable that the drive of these so elaborately aimed cosmic missiles among our chromosomes would be to increase the intellectual power of the Martianized individuals very greatly. There seemed to be no alternative to that conclusion. And for some very deep-seated reason in his make-up, it was an intolerable thought for him, that there should appear any class of creatures on earth intellectually above his own, unless they were profoundly inferior to him morally, and so repulsive and ugly as practically to reverse the handicap against him. They had to be ugly in appearance, they had to be ugly in motive and action. There had to be that compensation at least. This idea of their ugliness followed the idea of their intelligence with such an air of necessity that it was some weeks before he began even to suspect that the two ideas might be separated.

At first he pictured a Martian as something hunched together, like an octopus, tentacular, saturated with evil poisons, oozing unpleasant juices, a gigantic leathery bladder of hate.[41] The smell, he thought, would be terrible. And those indirect offspring who were to be so foully disseminated upon earth, were bound, he imagined, to be not simply intelligent in a hard unsympathetic way but in some manner disfigured and disgusting. They would be bound to have turnip heads, bladder-of-lard crania, shortsighted eyes, horrible little faces, long detestable hands, unathletic and possibly crippled bodies. . . .

Yet struggling desperately against this trend were certain vague apprehensions about his wife and child.

2

There was an extraordinary division in his mind at this time. Two cognate currents of suspicion ran side by side and would not mingle.

His wife was at once associated with and separated from his general line of thought. If, for instance, Dr Holdman Stedding had asked him outright, "Do you think your wife is one of these people who have been touched in their natal phase by the magic of the cosmic vibrations?" he would have answered at once with almost perfect honesty that these Martian speculations of his had absolutely nothing to do with her. But he would not have answered the question calmly; he would have had a touch of defensive indignation in his voice. And it was not a question he would have asked himself. It was a question he could not have asked himself; there was some barrier against that.

He was resisting a very obvious impulse to complete the link of association and fear that linked his long-standing sense of some strangeness about his wife, with this Martian idea. The two lines of suggestions were in reality connected and consecutive, but by some self-protective necessity he would not see that his extreme readiness to accept the suggestion of a Martian influx had any direct relation to his long-incubated sense of the elfin quality of his wife. They were groups of ideas in different spheres.

But these spheres, of which the Martian one was now spinning so busily, were drawing closer and closer together in his mind. Within a measurable time they were bound to collide, to coalesce into one common whirlpool, which might be a very tumbled whirlpool indeed. Then he would be bound to face the realization that had already projected itself in his words to the doctor: "so that presently our very children may not prove to be our own."

This intimation, breaking through his resistances evoked first the dread of an abnormal child, prematurely wise, macrocephalic, with dreadful tentacular hands. . . . So his essential humanity presented the thing. If the thing was a monster, what should he do?

He thought of doing some very dreadful things.

Such nightmare ideas haunted him more and more distressingly until the birth of his child. The immediate advent of that event filled him with almost uncontrollable terror. By an immense effort he concealed it and behaved himself.

He was amazed—even Dr Holdman Stedding was amazed—to have the young man brought into the world after a labour of less than an hour. No monstrous struggle. No frightful crisis. No Caesarean operation.

"Is he—is he *all right?*" he asked incredulous.

"Fit as a fiddle," said Dr Holdman Stedding almost boisterously. Because he had found something contagious in the father's uneasiness.

"No malformations? No strangeness?"

"On my honour, Mr Davis, you don't deserve such a child! You don't. When they've done a little washing you shall see it. I'm not often enthusiastic. I've seen too many of 'em."

And it looked indeed a perfect little creature. When they put it into his parental arms a great wave of instinctive tenderness surged up in the heart of Joseph Davis. Like endless fathers in his position before him, he was overcome by the wonderful fact that the creature's little hands had perfect nails and fingers.

Why had he ever been afraid?

"I feel I'd like to see her," he said.

"Not just yet. A little while yet. Though she's doing splendidly."

Whereupon Dr Holdman Stedding said a slightly unfortunate thing: "There's not a painted Madonna in all the world with a lovelier bambino than hers."

Mr Joseph Davis's expression became thoughtful.

Silently he handed back his precious burden to the hovering nurse.

He was minded to go out and not to see Mary for a time.

Then by a great effort he overcame this impulse and stayed indoors in his study downstairs, and presently he was taken in to her, and when he saw her, tired but flushed and triumphant, with the child laid close to her, some long-standing restraint seemed to break between them and he called her his darling and knelt down beside her, weeping.

"Dear Joe!" she said, and her hand crept out and ruffled his hair gently. "Queer Joe!"

3

After that his ideas about the quality of the Martians' influences and purposes began to change. After all, the two streams of realization came together in his mind gently and naturally, and he felt with the completest assurance and with no lingering trace of horror that both his wife and his child belonged to this new order of human beings that was appearing upon the planet.

After that it was that his researches, which at the beginning had been directed mainly to Poor Law institutions for defective and malformed children, asylums, wonder children, and the more grotesque arcana of gynaecology, turned rather to schools and universities and the ascertainable characteristics of exceptional and gifted people. He passed from a hunt for monsters to an investigation of outstanding endowment, to the detection and analysis of what is called genius in every field of human activity. He brooded over the pictured riddles of Dürer, he read the notebooks of Leonardo.[42] He found a new interest in symbolic art and in whatever moody and inexplicable decoration from remote times and places came to his attention. Were these enigmas like cries in the dark, the struggling intimations of novel reactions and novel attitudes on the part of Martian pioneers towards the customs and traditions of our world?

He had never told any one, least of all would he have told Dr Holdman Stedding, that dreams about Martians were becoming rather frequent with him. They were extremely consistent dreams or at least they were pervaded with a sense of consistency. These dream-Martians were no longer repulsive creatures, grotesques and caricatures, and yet their visible appearance was not human. They had steadfast, dark eyes, very widely separated, and their mouths were still and resolute. Their broad brows and round heads made him think of the smooth wise-looking heads of seals and cats and he could not distinguish clearly whether they had shadowy hands and arms or tentacles. There was always a lens-like effect about his vision, as though he saw them through the eyepiece of some huge optical instrument.[43] Ripples passed across the lens and increased the indistinctness, and ever and again flickering bunches of what he assumed were cosmic rays exploded from nothingness across the picture and flashed out radiating to the periphery and vanished. He felt that his dreams were taking him into a world where our ideas of form and process, of space and time, are no longer valid. In his dreams it was not as if he went across space to Mars, it was as if a veil became translucent.

Once or twice in the daytime he had tried to make sketches of these watchers, but their physical forms had always eluded his pencil. He had never been able to draw very well, but also he had a feeling that even for a skilled artist there would have been difficulties about the planes and dimensions of these beings.

Moreover not only was he finding this difficulty in determining a Martian form but he was finding a parallel difficulty in fixing any common characteristics for the earthly types he was beginning to distinguish as "Martianized." All that they had in common was that they were "different" and that this difference involved a certain detachment from common reactions. They lived apart. They thought after their own fashion. He was not sure whether they were actually insusceptible to mass emotions; he may have expected them to be, and that with him would have been half-way to thinking them so.

4

On this visit to Gorpel he pursued what was becoming his usual technique. It was at once subtle and a trifle crazy. There was a streak of masochism about it. He had written all his books so far to appeal to the heroic common humanity in all of us. And now he was using the same stuff to eliminate, so to speak, common humanity. He was looking for minds that did not respond.

He had brought down a lecture that had always proved extremely successful with ordinary schoolboys, "The Grandeur that was Rome." In this he unfolded his tale of the heroic patriots who stud the Latin tradition, from Horatius defending the Bridge, to Caesar crowning the great task of the Republic by annexing it to British history, Octavius creating the Empire and Justinian giving us Roman Law. It was a procession of statuesque figures, more or less clean-shaven and for most part in togas, evoking as they passed a fungoid growth of unnecessary aqueducts, corpulent amphitheatres and Corinthian columns, and conferring on the whole world the blessings of the Pax Romana. The Punic Wars, with a faint flavouring of Anti-Semitism, too faint to be disagreeable, he presented as a gigantic necessary struggle between noble north-side soldiers and revengeful, obdurate, but extremely competent south-side loanmongers. He ignored every reality of hate, suspicion, greed, panic and brutish cruelty that characterized that monstrous mutual destruction of the Mediterranean civilizations, the Punic Wars, and still less did he let those essential features of the mighty Pax, the omnipresent cross for rebels and the omnipresent tax-collector for every one, peep out from behind those glorious Roman arches. As he orated this familiar discourse he watched the boys. A few, incapable of attention, were inattentive, but the discipline of the school was good and their inattention was passive. The majority were responsive. They drank in the mighty fable. Their eyes betrayed their imaginative excitement. Their faces became nobler, stern. They became conquering generals subduing barbarians, pro-consuls assuaging the bickerings of subject races.[44]

It was an answer to trumpets that stirred in them. It was what he had heard someone call the "Onward, Christian Soldiers"[45] reaction.

With all that Davis was familiar. But now he was looking for scepticism and intelligent dissent.

There was one little fellow sitting up near the corner who from the start he felt assured was Martianized. He had untidy hair and a shrewd faintly humorous white face, and he listened throughout, cheek on hand, very attentively and with a questioning expression. He heard, untouched. The real Martian quality.

"That's my boy *here*," said Davis and inquired about him afterwards.

"A queer little chap," said the headmaster. "A queer little chap. Behaves pretty well, but he's somehow disappointing. Doesn't *throw* himself *into* things. A streak of something very nearly amounting to—well, scepticism. Yet his people are quite decent people and the Dean of Clumps is his uncle. He asks questions no other boy would think of. The other day he asked, what is *spiritual*?"

"Well," said Mr Davis after a thoughtful pause, "what *is* spiritual?"

"But need I tell *you* of all people?"

"What did you tell him? I'm finding a sort of difficulty in putting this in a chapter I am writing about the saintly life."

The headmaster of Gorpel did not answer the question immediately. Instead he went on to say in a slightly offended voice: "I find all my normal boys understand the word without discussion, take it for granted. Spiritual—Material, a natural opposition. One ascends, the other gravitates. There it is, plain as a pikestaff. No need to discuss it."

"Unless some little—toad, like that, asks the question point-blank."

"He refuses to see. Why, he said, should we make a sort of extract of reality and call it spirituality and pretend the two things are primary opposites?"

"He said that! Rather—subtle."

"Too subtle for a boy of his age. Unwholesome."

"But spirit isn't an extract, is it?"

"So I said to him. 'Life,' he said, 'seems to me just one, Sir. I can't think of it in any other way. Sorry, Sir, I've tried.'"

"He said that—that he couldn't think in any other way? That's very interesting. How did you meet that?"

"In his particular case I explained by means of illustrations."

"And he was satisfied?"

"Not in the least. He criticized my illustrations. Rather penetratingly, I admit. He wanted me to define. But you see, Mr Davis, the fundamental things of life cannot be defined. He made me realize that more clearly than I have ever done before. All the great fundamentals, Deity, Eternity—Faith in What?—it is as if there was a sort of holy of holies beyond the reach of exact definitions. So it seems to me. It is useless, I find, to argue about them. It robs our attitudes of dignity . . . robs *them* of dignity. . . . We are reduced to logic-chopping. Quibbles. . . . We understand by intuition what we mean and what other people mean. Best to leave it at that."

"And you told him if he didn't understand what spiritual meant, not to go on thinking about it yet but wait."

"And pray," said the headmaster of Gorpel. "In effect I said that. In effect. Not exactly. Not too definitely. One must go carefully. Afterwards I made him learn Corinthians One thirteen[46] by heart—not as if it was exactly an answer but as if it threw a light—and I hope it did him good."

"You don't know?"

"I don't know. There are elusive matters, Mr Davis. A boy who wants to argue must not be indulged too far. There are limits."

"I wonder," said Mr Davis, feeling his way carefully, "if perhaps *types*—types like this youngster may really be something more than merely obstinate. Whether by some instinctive necessity, by some difference in themselves they may not find something—some inacceptable lack of fineness, some lack of clearness, in various distinctions, we assume, distinctions we *have* assumed and which we make by habit. . . ."

"I can't entertain thoughts like that," said the headmaster abruptly. "I cannot conduct the work of this great school and prepare my regiment of youngsters year by year for their attack on life and responsibility, if I am also to carry on an examination of the fundamental values we set on things."

"But if presently instead of one inassimilable boy you find half a dozen of him turning up—or a score?"

The headmaster looked at his visitor. "I devoutly hope not, Mr Davis," he said. "I devoutly hope not. You are giving me food—not for thought—no!—for nightmares. . . ."

"Now here, now there," said Mr Davis as he stood on the headmaster's doorstep. "Certainly that boy is one of them. They don't see life as we see it. They can't think of it in our way. And they make us begin to doubt that we see it ourselves as we have always imagined we did."

CHAPTER 7

The World Begins to
Hear about the Martians

1

It is almost impossible to trace how this realization that mankind, under the spur of the cosmic rays, was launched upon a career of genetic change, seeped from the minds of the first discoverers, Laidlaw, that rufous man in the Planetarium Club (to whom it seemed no more than a passing freak of fancy), Mr Davis (who was first to take it seriously), Dr Holdman Stedding, and Professor Ernest Keppel, into the general consciousness. But a few weeks after the birth of Mary's child, an article appeared in the *Weekly Refresher* from the pen of that admirable scientific popularizer, Harold Rigamey, in which, as Professor Keppel rather inelegantly put it, he "completely spilt the beans."

It is possible that Rigamey got the thing at second or third hand from Dr Holdman Stedding, who oddly enough seems to have been the least discreet of all that primary group. Dr Stedding may have described it to one or two fellow-practitioners as an example of the extreme intellectual elaboration that may appear in a case of delusional insanity. There is no evidence that Laidlaw, after his first imaginative outbreak, ever gave the matter a second thought until he got the echo in the newspapers. But he may very well have repeated his fantasy on some after-dinner occasion. He was the last survivor of the old Bob Stevenson, York Powell,[47] school of talk, a gorgeous talker.

Harold Rigamey was a peculiarly constituted being, he had a mind that did not so much act as react. He was a born ultra-heretic. He disbelieved everything and then doubled back on his disbelief. From a sound historical and literary training he had recoiled in a state of unsympathetic curiosity to science and had achieved a very respectable position on the literary side of journalism by writing about science in a manner that caused the greatest discomfort and perplexity to men of science. He found wonders for them when they saw nothing wonderful and incredible triumphs of paradox in their simplest statements. He mated them to the strangest associates.

He had an infuriating openmindedness to every unorthodox extravagance. He hated dogma and he was full of faith. He was always reconciling science and religion, spiritualism and behaviourism, medicine and Christian Science, and this reconciling disposition won him quite a large following of readers eager to keep their mental peace amidst the vast, the incongruous, alarming and sometimes far too urgent suggestions of our modern world.

They were all a little uneasy with him and that was a part of his charm. There were stimulants in all his sedatives. When he asked his readers to come and meet spiritual worth, they were never quite sure whether that meant the dear Archbishop of Canterbury, all clean and scented with his pretty purple-and-red evening clothes, his pretty lace cuffs, his pretty Episcopal ring, and his general vacuous urbanity, or whether it meant a rather repellent, though no doubt equally edifying, encounter with some unsanitarily pure and indecently stark fakir on a bed of nails; and when he remarked upon the stern veracities of science, whether it would be a fresh explosion in the mathematical engine-room, a vitamin of incredible potency, or a breathing exercise from America that at once confirmed and completed the remarkable inhalations of ancient Tibet, he had in mind. For some time Harold Rigamey had been working out in his own mind some sort of linkage of interplanetary communications with the all too neglected science of astrology; he thought he might make something quite exciting out of it, and this weird idea of Laidlaw's came to him like the voice of the Lord to a Hebrew prophet.

For some time he had been feeling that his characteristic methods of popularizing science were no longer growing in popular favour. Men of science are a peculiar, an almost ungracious class, and very often the more you popularize them the less they like it. Maybe it was a public realization of their lack of appreciation for Harold Rigamey's services, or maybe it was just a surfeit of subtle but occasionally very incomprehensible wonders, that was affecting the first abundant public response to Harold Rigamey; at any rate he felt that his popularity was dimmer than it used to be. A really new and exciting topic, that only needed a little care and thought in the handling to go far and wide, was just the tonic he had been requiring.

Mindful of the faint elements of insecurity in his own credit he set about the subject with considerable skill and discretion. He first informed his public through a couple of articles, called *The Voice of the Stars*, of a "growing realization" that "extra-terrestrial forces of some unknown kind" were "indubitably" attempting to establish communication with our planet. He invoked almost every known authority upon extra-terrestrial radiations, produced in a skilfully clipped form some rare unguarded statements by eminent professors, promoted one or two rash speculations by obscure people in remote parts of the earth to a distinguished scientific standing, and invented a few anonymous scientists of his own. (Some day *Nature* will have to publish a list of otherwise non-existent scientists, available for public controversy.)

"Scientists tell us" was a very favourite phrase with Harold Rigamey. He wrote of "numerous efforts" which he said had been made to "discover codes" in these extra-terrestrial radiations and of the growing conviction of "scientists" of all sorts and shades and sizes, in the existence of these persistent attempts to attract our attention from outside our world.

"This present century," wrote Harold Rigamey, "already goes far beyond its predecessor, the Century of Invention. This is the Century of Discovery. The sixteenth century was a Century of Terrestrial Discovery; but this is the Century of Extra-Terrestrial discovery. Already the immortality of the soul, or at any rate persistence after death, seems to be experimentally established, and now we realize upon the most convincing evidence that man is not alone on his planet; he is a citizen in what may prove to be an abundantly populated universe."

Eminent men of science read Harold Rigamey's latest revelation of what science is doing in a mood of apoplectic fury. "What are we to do about this sort of thing?" they said to their wives at breakfast and their wives said: "My dear, *what* can you do?" And there the matter ended. The mystical mathematicians with their expanding and contracting universes, Relativity-exponents and the like retired from the arena of popular attention like a small group of concertina players on the entry of a large brass band. An unprecedented mail informed Harold

Rigamey of the successful opening of his campaign. His next stage was to go on to the *Fantastic Connexion of Cosmic Rays and Human Mutations* and then straightaway to *The Martian Genes* and *The Martian Type* and so told the whole story as we have already seen it unfolding in the mind of Mr Joseph Davis, but with a richness of confirmatory detail altogether beyond our modest record of actualities.

2

The reception of the astounding revelation was ample and inconclusive and it afforded Professor Keppel considerable scope for his gift for bitter comment. Popular intelligence, the professor pointed out to the acquiescent Dr Holdman Stedding, has long since ceased to attach any real importance to concrete statements except in so far as they concern football and cricket results, and winners of races and (with caution and reservations) stock-exchange quotations. Outside this definite range of immediate rational interests it has achieved an almost complete toleration, an inactive indifference, to any statement whatever. "You may tell the public anything you like nowadays," said Keppel, "and it will not care a rap. It is not that it disbelieves; it is not that it believes; but that its belief apparatus has been over-strained and misused beyond any sort of reaction, positive or negative, to the things that it is told.

"Consider the," he expatiated, "—we will not say *contents*—of the average human mind today; but consider the things that are lying about side by side upon that flaccid expanse of mentality." (Dr Holdman Stedding repeated these precious words silently; "flaccid expanse of mentality.") "It has been told a beautiful story of Creation, the Garden of Eden and the Fall. It does not know whether that story is a fable, a parable or a statement of fact, and manifestly it does not care. If Sir Leonard Woolley and Mr H. V. Morton[48] announced a joint discovery of Eden, raised a restoration fund and provided tourist facilities at reasonable rates, the public would go in a state of inscrutable acquiescence and enormous numbers, to visit the ancestral garden-plot. And at the same time in the same brain, so to speak, this public has accepted a great mass of statement to the effect that it is descended, through something called Evolution, from gorilla-like ancestors. It would be quite capable of visiting in the morning the veritable scene where six or seven thousand years ago Eve, surrounded by all the latest novelties of Creation, her wedding presents, so to speak, accepted the apple from the serpent, and then of inspecting a caveful of fifty-thousand-year-old Neanderthaler remains in the afternoon. It has lost all sense of incongruity. It has lost all sense of relevance. It neither rejects nor assimilates nor correlates anything. It believes everything and it believes nothing.

"In effect," said Mr Keppel, "it does nothing about anything at all. There is no conceivable issue now upon which it can be roused to spontaneous action. If it opened its newspaper one morning and read that Christianity has been abolished, it would wonder what sort of pensions the bishops would get—'pretty fat, I expect'—and then turn over to see if the cross-word puzzle was an easy one. If it read that the queer noises it had heard in the night were the trumpets announcing the Resurrection and the end of the world for tomorrow afternoon, it would probably remark that the buses and tubes were full enough as it was without all these Dead coming up, and that a thing of that sort ought to be held somewhere abroad where there was more room. . . ."

In America the disclosure of the Martian intervention was received with bright incredulity. Rigamey's articles were syndicated everywhere and credited nowhere. It is a popular error, Keppel insisted, that Americans are more accessible to ideas than the British. Notions indeed they are never averse to. Notions are different. A notion is something you can handle. But an idea, a general idea, has a way of getting all over you and subjugating you, and no free spirit submits to that. Confronted with an idea the American says: "Oh, yeah!" or "Sez you" and the Englishman says: "I don't fink," or at a higher social level "Piffle—piffle before the wind." These simple expressions are as good against ideas as the sign of the cross used to be against the mediaeval devil. The pressure is at once relieved.

But your American has none of the Englishman's ability to ignore. After having said his "Sez you" or "Oh, yeah" and killed an idea, your American is only too ready to make light of the corpse. His joy in caricature and extravaganza is as vast as his sense of reality is deficient. So that Harold Rigamey's revelations, relieved of all terror of actuality and being vigorously syndicated, went widely and swiftly through the thought and phraseology of those quick-witted millions. "Are you a Martian?" was on the cars within a week of the syndication of Harold's last article and "Don't appeal to my Martian side" had become a conversational counter in circulation from coast to coast. A new caricaturist started a series of Martian cartoons in the *New Yorker* that caught on at once and were very widely imitated. The music-halls were brisk rather than clever in taking up the idea. Along a thousand divergent channels flowed the fertilizing suggestion and evoked a weedy jungle of responses. "Dry Martians" became the dominant cocktail. Hundreds of deeply preoccupied Negroes pranced and flung themselves about in the Southern sunshine in search of a real Martian Newstep. Thousands of industrious advertisement designers spent sleepless nights subduing the new idea in this way and that way to the varied uses of their calling.

And Harold Rigamey turned his pen to other things.

3

The only real attempt to deal with the coming of the Martians upon a serious scale was made on the British side, and it was made by no less a person than Lord Thunderclap, that great synthetic press peer. It was made against the advice of his most trusted associates and it failed.

Lord Thunderclap was one of the supreme successes of the journalistic and business world; he had become enormously rich and influential in a gigantic inaccurate way all out of nasty little periodicals, and he was quite intelligent enough to understand there must be something wrong about his headlong, unchallenged prominence. Both he and his slightly derisive rival and associate Lord Bendigo,[49] deep down in their very bright minds, had that same sense of haphazard expansion and unjustifiable eminence; they could not believe, however much they tried, that in the long run the world would not call them to account; they had none of the innate assurance of royal personages and born aristocrats, and they were both haunted by the feeling that sooner or later, something hard, stern, and powerful, a Sphinx, a Nemesis, would come round a corner upon them and unfold an indictment for immediate attention, asking them what they thought they were and what in the last resort they thought they were up to.

The mercurial Bendigo regarded that possibility with unaffected facetiousness but Thunderclap was made of less mobile stuff. He liked being the large massive thing he was; the longer he lived the more he wanted to believe in his own importance and feel that he was really true. The longer he lived the more he liked himself and the less could he bear that sense of a delayed but pursuing judgement. He could ill endure this unprotesting acquiescence of this world in him; the accumulated menace of its uncritical disregard; but even less now could he endure the thought that this toleration might end.

The dark other-world of insomnia added itself to his daylight existence. That awful Court of Enquiry without any definite charges, just asking what he was and why, sat there in perpetual unprogressive session, waiting—waiting for something. There was no hurry. Most terrifyingly there was no hurry. But what could they be saving up for him? Day after day he went about his large abundant life, being the great Lord Thunderclap—because what else on earth could he be? What else on earth could he do? The day passed into evening, evening to night and so at last to bed. And then that insatiable question. . . . What net were they weaving?

The faces about him were polite masks. You challenged them: "You were saying about me—?"

"I said nothing, my lord."

He told nobody of this increasing obsession, but the existence of his profound uneasiness was more or less manifest to most of his associates and subordinates. Was there something that had never been found out? They tried to guess at that. But nothing definite appeared; it was a dread at large. Evidently he feared men of science and knowledge, especially men who were reputed to be profoundly and exceptionally versed in political and social and economic affairs. What must they really think of his journalistic influence, his activities in party matters, his financial affairs? Were they just quietly letting him have rope, sewing him up unobtrusively? And he suspected the civil service profoundly. These civil servants, he thought, knew more than was good for them already and they were always trying to know more. The word "inspector" moved him to a pallid rage. "More Inspectors!" was one of the shrillest screams in his multifarious publications. Nasty mean men he insisted these inspectors were, with sharp noses like foxes, needy dependants, and a passion for petty bribes; always peeping through keyholes they were, looking into windows, creeping up pipes, getting through gratings, weaving a net about all wholesome business enterprise. They had to be fought off. They had to be frustrated, denounced, caricatured at every turn. And all these Trade Union and Labour people wanting to know, perpetually wanting to know, and then, I suppose, interfere. And this London School of Economics![50] What were they putting together and plotting and planning there? What did they want to have a school of economics for anyhow? It was like marking the cards.

In Lord Thunderclap's mind socialism was another name for malignant investigation. He had no idea what harmless, disconnected, doctrinaire little creatures socialists are, and how limited an area of the social problem they have ever explored. He really thought they had a strong, clear plan for a workable human society all ready for use, a hard competent society, ready to thrust him and his like out of existence. At any time now they might spring it upon him. He fought wildly in the darkness against that persuasion, but it held him. He was probably the only man alive in England who believed in socialism to that extent.

In his perpetual attempt to materialize his terror he mixed up all these professors, civil servants, inspectors, socialists, sociologists (whom he regarded as a nastier variety of socialist), liberals—every sort of interrogator and critic—in a great jumble of hateful menace, the "Intelligentsia," the "Lefts," the "Reds." He imagined a world-wide, hostile, incredibly subtle, incredibly far-sighted net closing about him. And he never really got them plain for a straight fight to a finish and have done with it. Never could he drag them into the light of open day. He knew that they were at it, at it all the time, conspiring, scheming, taking their orders, passing their messages, nodding, winking, giving their signals, working their mischiefs. They ramified everywhere. You never knew who was with them. They were Jesuits today and freemasons tomorrow. Even judges and lawyers might be scheming. Hard to deal with them. You were safe with no one.

All his partners and secretaries and editors knew those odd moments of his, when he would affect to look out of the window idly, and then spin round upon you with incredible nimbleness to scrutinize your face.

Or when he would lead you through a long rambling talk about Russia, about Germany, about China, to jump upon you suddenly with a handful of carefully premeditated posers, designed to wring the very plotting soul out of you.

Such was the large fear-obsessed mentality to which the disclosures of Harold Rigamey came like a torch to a hayrick.

Never for a moment when he heard it did Lord Thunderclap doubt the story. Not until he read about it in his own papers had he a twinge of doubt. It came as the embodiment and confirmation of his worst fears. He felt he had really known all about it from the very beginning. He carried Harold Rigamey off for dinner and the night to his suburban headquarters at Castle Windrow, Bunting Hayland, and thither he assembled by wire and telephone all his most trusted henchmen, tools, stooges, subordinates, intimates, Watsons, yes-girls, medical advisers, soothsayers, astrologists, stenographers, masseurs, soothers and family connexions.

"The thing's out at last," he said. "Listen to him! Listen to what Rigamey has to tell us. We've been barking up the wrong tree. These Reds—Moscow—Bernard Shaw[51]—New Dealers—Atheists—Protocols of Zion,[52] all of that—mere agents. It's *Mars* that is after us. Listen to him. Mars! What are we to do about it? What are we to do?

"Everything we value in life. Cross and crown. Nation and loyalty. Morals. Christmas. Family life. The Reds are just their front line. While we stand about here and stare at each other and do nothing, there they are working away, getting born, growing up, plotting, planning—one after another—these monsters. I ask you. Is nothing to be done?"

"Well, Chief," said Cotton-Jones, the arch-soother. "Everything has to be done. But it's got to be done in the right way. No need to tell *you* that."

"The whole world is in danger. Hideous danger."

"That's too big for stop-press news. Chief, we've got to go into conference right away. Here and now. We've got to just hold the whole thing in silence, until we've organized a plan of campaign and a general staff. You said it, Chief, yourself, years ago. 'The more urgent the crisis,' you said, 'the more danger there is in hurry.'"

"I said that?" said Lord thunderclap.

"Yes, Sir. You said that. . . ."

It was daylight before that assembly at Castle Windrow dispersed and Lord Thunderclap was safely put to bed. His sedatives were furtively doubled. And throughout all the offices and organizations which owed him allegiance, grave and weary men plotted guardedly with each other—no double-crossing mind!—against the call for action that would come to them when he awoke.

Cotton-Jones, toiling wearily up to his suite under the roof at headquarters, realized suddenly the mysterious sensitiveness of the Thunderclap system. Two small lift attendants stopped upon the second landing to exchange news, unaware of his presence in the middle elevator. The youngest and shrillest spoke without emotion.

"Jimmy, you heard? The Chief's nuts at last."

"Clean off it?"

"Clean."

"Bound to happen sooner or later. What dislodged him?"

"Them Martians. . . ."

Now how had the little devils got hold of that? . . .

Throughout the most difficult ten days in their lives the entourage of Lord Thunderclap struggled to mitigate the impact of his full excitement upon the public. What he had in mind seemed to be some sort of world-wide witch-smelling for Martians everywhere. He swept aside every difficulty there might be in distinguishing them. You could tell them by the things they said and the way they behaved. You could tell them because instinctively you disliked them. . . . Not a massacre. Massacres were out of date. What was needed was a vast sanitary concentration of all these people to save our race (Lord Thunderclap) alive.

Rigamey had brought some entirely irrelevant facts about what are called Mongoloid children into the discussion, and Thunderclap seized upon them as data for the first selection of victims in this world-drive against the Martians. Individuals of this type should be at once arrested and secluded in protective isolation. There ought to be a human race-purity conference set up in permanent session. All the leading obstetricians in the world ought to be in it, with stimulating fees and unlimited powers.

Like to like. It was natural for the turbid stream of Anti-Semitism to contribute some richly helpful ideas to his fresh flow of anti-Martian animosity. . . .

Cotton-Jones took his courage in both hands and withstood his master. "We can't do this," he said, with the Chief's programme in his hand.

"We can't do this? Then what on earth *are* we to do?"

"The public mind is not prepared for anything of the sort."

His lordship raged up and down the room but Cotton-Jones felled him with the deadliest, most arresting assertion that an editorial assistant can use.

"It will fall *flat*," said Cotton-Jones.

"This!?"

"It will fall *flat*."

"We can't go on with this on our own responsibility," he insisted and Thunderclap knew that he was right. "We must have authority. We must quote. We ourselves cannot seem to be bringing this out from the office. Merely from the office. Journalistic stunt, they will say. Yes, Sir. They will say that. Newspapers may lead but they should not appear to lead. We must seem to be responding to 'publicly responsible, unquestionable appeals.' *Your* words, Chief. Someone not ourselves, someone else, must make for righteousness."

He shook the programme in his hand. He added a still more difficult assertion.

"And really—for a thing of this size—we must bring in other groups of papers."

"I have had something of that sort in mind throughout," said Thunderclap after a stupendous pause.

He walked across the room. "Perhaps I have been precipitate. I see things too quickly."

He sat down to his desk and began to write down, strike out, and tick off names. There were one or two great physicians on the verge of advertisement; they ought to give him something. After all he had done for them. No. Damn them, they wouldn't. One or two of the more pushful young bishops were still in the toady stage, still rather anxious to prove how serviceable and friendly they could be to any lord of publicity. They surely might be called upon to denounce this diabolical threat to mankind. He sent them urgent and embarrassing communications, held them up himself on the telephone, and found them as blandly evasive as they knew how. They knew very well how. He cast about for this great public figure and then that to shoulder the new burthen. Gradually, as he sought, with diminishing success, among these great instruments of public stimulation, the pressure of his own initiative dispersed itself. Fatigue supervened. Violence deferred maketh the heart grow sick.[53] Four, five, six days passed and nothing stupendous was done. In the life of Lord Thunderclap two days are a thousand years.[54] The bright surface of his great disclosure was dulled by familiarity. The preparatory articles, announcements, and so forth became less and less a preparation and more and more like the wailing and booming of a receding school of ichthyosaurii heard through the twilight of the past.

It came to him abruptly one night that he didn't care a damn now if nothing was done. The affair had evaporated. If nobody cared to stir a finger, the whole silly business might slide. The Martians might *eat* the world now so far as he was concerned. It would last his time—anyhow. What was the sense of being the one earnest energetic man in a world of unresponsive fools?

He called Cotton-Jones into his presence. "You've been going too strong on this Martian stuff," he said, and Cotton-Jones knew at once that the brainstorm was over. "You've made it a bit too loud and brassy. The public doesn't want to hear about them in this serious way you've been putting it. They want it guyed.[55] What the public won't hear about can't exist really. Circulation dies down and then where are you? Ease off on it. Guy it."

"After all we have said!" reflected Cotton-Jones.

"Ease off on it. Make it kind of semi-symbolical—humorous and all that."

"I get you," said Cotton-Jones, trying not to look too glad. "I think I can manage to ease it off. Yes, it's a damned good political nickname,

106

Chief, whatever you like to say. You've never thought of anything better. Give 'Highbrow' and 'Brain Trust' a holiday for the next ten years. Let the Reds fade out. *Martians!* People will hate them from the word Go!"

4

Mr Joseph Davis stood at the upper corner of Trafalgar Square watching the westward flow of buses below. A number of them were carrying huge starry advertisement boards with a new inscription. He could make out three capital M's but he had to look hard before he could read the intervening letters. They spelled out "Musical Martian Midgets."

"That's how they see it," said Mr Davis. "H'm."

His eyes were lifted sharply by a challenging flash across the twilight blue. A sky sign took up the words in letters of raw red fire, "Musical Martian Midgets." . . .

"And all the same," whispered Mr Davis after some moments of silent reflection, "*they are here.*"

CHAPTER 8
How these Star Begotten People may Presently Get Together

1

"So your Martians are coming after all, Davis," said Dr Holdman Stedding.

"I've given you my facts," said Mr Davis, "a new sort of human being is appearing. Of that I am convinced. . . . I never said they were Martians."

"The name's got into the story. And after all, you know—they may be."

"Why not the star-men?" said Keppel. "*Homo sideralis?* How would one say *Star Begotten* as a specific adjective?"

"One name seems to be as good as another," said Davis, affecting indifference. "Until we know better what they are, why trouble about the name? Let us stick to Martians."

"The newspapers have no doubt about it. Either there are Martians, they insist, or there is nothing."

Davis shrugged his shoulders.

"On the whole I wish this hadn't leaked out to the press," said Mr Keppel, crouching upon his arms over his mahogany and looking malignantly intelligent. "Marvellous how the press can make almost anything—unbelievable. What has the press made of it? First this Thunderclap boom. Then general derision. Then general disregard. Nothing stales so rapidly as a new popular idea. What have we now? General indifference. A few pathetic believers run about, half ashamed of themselves, and assert their faith by starting silly-looking little special periodicals and societies. I am told there are at least two pro-Martian societies in London, and three against. The people who produce that pink-covered journal called *Welcome* seem to be the chief. In America there are quite a lot of associations, I'm told, but all small. Most of them have a tendency to amalgamate with occultists and mix up Mars with Tibet. Then a new type of delusional insanity has appeared. God Almighty, it seems, is out of fashion among our lunatics. They are all Martians nowadays and most of them are Kings or Emperors of Mars. What else has come out of your great disclosure? Ourselves—we *toughs*, who knew all along just how much there was in it, and were too wise to shout."

He looked sideways at Davis from under his overhanging brow.

"You believe really—?" asked Davis.

Keppel would neither assent nor deny.

"No one would believe what we in our bones feel to be the reality. We're not quite sure—but we feel it. We're not quite definite but a reality is there. It *is* unbelievable. So why incur suspicion and contempt by talking about it? Nothing is to be done. We cannot control what is happening. We cannot avert it. Here they come. Here we are."

2

"I want to talk about it," said Keppel. "I want badly to talk about it."

"I find myself thinking about it a lot," said Dr Holdman Stedding.

"I think now of nothing else," said Davis.

It seemed to him that Keppel had got this Martian fever now almost as badly as himself. That grotesque, distorted dark face was flushed, and every gesture suggested the repression of a profound excitement. But Keppel's resolve to control the stir in his imagination and to keep things as matter-of-fact as possible was very evident.

The three men were dining at Keppel's house for the express purpose of receiving and discussing the first results of Davis's investigations.

"Let's see how far we have got," said Keppel. "Let us try to disentangle as far as we can the pure guess-fantasy of an extra-terrestrial intervention, from the established realities that Davis has been elucidating. A new sort of mind is coming into the world, with a new, simpler, clearer, and more powerful way of thinking. That I think is manifest. It has already got into operation individually here and there and produced a sort of disorder of innovation in human affairs. But so far these new minds haven't got together for any sort of associated living.

So far. They are hardly aware of themselves, much less of each other. They are scattered about anyhow. . . . All that, I think, seems to be established? . . ."

Mr Davis nodded assent.

"These new types have made their presence felt as yet, chiefly through discoveries in material science and mechanical invention. At this present stage they are too scattered and isolated for novel social inventions. That sort of thing requires extensive co-operations. It is on a different plane. These newcomers are dispersed; they are not appearing in bunches; they do not even know that they are a peculiar people; each one of them has been deeply embedded, so to speak, in the circumstances of his or her own birth. From birth they have all been presented with established views of the world and compelled to adjust their social behaviour to established institutions. Many no doubt have been completely baffled by the dogmatic unreason of the normal human arrangements in which they found themselves *set*. In—what shall I say?—in human affairs, they've never had a chance so far. But in regard to *things*, mere things, bits of glass, scraps of metal, springs and balances, they have not been encumbered to the same extent. There they have been able to think freely almost from the outset. . . .

"That has been the opening phase. Nobody has ever tried to explain the immense advance in scientific knowledge in the past century and a half—but this does explain it. There has been a great outbreak of precise mechanical discovery and invention. That meant—that means—a necessary discordance in human affairs—scattered inventions everywhere, a great forward drive, a revolutionary drive in mechanical science and a relative lag in social understanding. There is an almost complete inability to make new ideas in the latter field *real*. That is a tougher proposition altogether. I think it is easy to explain why that should be so. But there is the reason why every one nowadays is contrasting our material progress with what is called—how do the bishops put it?—our ethical and social backwardness. A temporary phase."

"But a damned unpleasant one," said Dr Holdman Stedding. "When the superman makes an aeroplane and the ape gets hold of it."

"Nevertheless—a *temporary* phase," continued Keppel, holding to his argument with resolute tenacity. "Because, as I say, to begin with these Martians have been rare and scattered. But as they become more numerous—and I assume that there is no reason whatever why they should not become more and more numerous—they will necessarily become aware of one another, and get into touch with one another. Such minds, following the line of least resistance, will gravitate to scientific work. They will note and classify mental types. This must lead almost directly to self-discovery. They will observe how they resemble each other and how they differ from the wimble-wamble of the common world. They will begin to know themselves for what they are."[56]

"A new chapter in history," said Mr Davis, contemplating it. "And then?"

"Let us think this out for a bit," said Keppel. "I believe a considerable amount of analysis of what is coming, is possible.[57] I think myself we can already make a rough forecast, but I shall feel much more certain about that when I have put what I have in mind before you two. If I get away with it. It does seem worth while to ask a few fairly obvious questions. What is going to be the next phase in this invasion? As these Martians multiply among us, they will, I assume, tend to crystallize out in some such way as I have indicated. They will develop a distinctively Martian view of life. They will begin to realize themselves for what they are, look for their own sort, feel their way towards a common understanding. They will emerge to social action in some fashion. . . . In what fashion?"

3

"But first of all," he said, "I want to clear up a preliminary matter —of some practical importance."

He concentrated on his hands spread out on the table before him. "I'd like to put it to Davis. Here we have, he says, a new kind of mind appearing in the world, a hard, clear, insistent mind. It used to appear at uncertain intervals. Rarely. It said: 'Why not?' and it made discoveries. Now apparently it is becoming—frequent. Not abundant as yet but frequent. Well, what I want to know is, is this new kind of mind when it appears, *complete*? Let me be perfectly plain about that. Certain genes in the human mentality, we agree, have been altered in this new type.

These new minds are harder, clearer, more essentially honest—yes. But are they completely detached from the old stuff or are they in many cases a sort of half-breed and all mixed up with it?

"I want to stress that half-breed idea. Are they so much human, human of the old pattern still, and so much—and only so much—clean Martian? So that one side of them is just the old system of self-regarding complexes, vanities, dear delusions—while the other side is like a crystal growing in mud? You see what I am after? It may not be true to talk as though we were dealing with human clay vis-à-vis with Martians. We are talking about human mud and against it we have to pit these partially liberated intelligences, still largely mixed with the old mud. All three of us have been in our various ways trying to get something like a real sense of what these new beings are. These new creatures—"

Keppel paused and looked at his hands. "They are going to be very tragic creatures. . . . In many cases. . . . What do you make of it, Davis? Of the half-breed idea?"

"I haven't seen it like that yet. You see, I have been going about trying to find certain lucid, intractable types. That was your suggestion, doctor. I've certainly found them. I've been looking for a sort of difference. . . ."

"You haven't thought of any other aspect?"

"No. . . . I haven't looked for resemblances, so to speak, in the difference," he added after a pause. "I've been looking for uncommon humanity; not for common humanity."

"Well," Keppel went on, talking chiefly to his intelligent-looking fingers, "that half-breed idea opens up a whole new world of considerations. It banishes Thunderclap's nightmare of a lot of little active hobgoblins swarming and multiplying and desecrating our homes and everything that has made human life *et cetera*. In the place of that sort of thing we have to suppose an increasing number of individuals scattered about the world, who, so far at any rate, never seem to have had a suspicion that they are not just ordinary human stuff. But who find life tremendously puzzling, much more puzzling than other people do. . . . Now perhaps—it will be different. . . .

"As children, like any other children, they will have begun by taking the world as they found it and believing everything they were told. Then as they grew up they would have found themselves mentally out of key. They would have found a disconcerting inconsistency about things in general. They would have thought at first that the abnormality was on the side of particular people about them and not on their own. They would have found themselves doubting whether their parents and teachers could possibly believe what they were saying. I think that among these Martians, that odd doubt—which many children nowadays certainly have—whether the whole world isn't some queer sort of put-up job and that it will all turn out quite differently presently—I think that streak of doubt would be an almost inevitable characteristic of them all."

"That doubt about the reality of what they are told?" considered Davis. "Children certainly have it. Even I . . ."

Keppel glanced at him for one half-instant.

"Now," said Keppel, still addressing his hands, "before I go on with these problems of what these Martians are going to do to our world, I would like to put some rather penetrating questions to myself and—both of you. You don't mind if I sort of lecture you? Or retail the obvious? I'm a professor in grain, you must remember."

Dr Holdman Stedding made assenting gestures and Davis remained obviously attentive.

"Let us try and make this room an apartment in the palace of truth for the time being. About ourselves . . . We are sane respectable citizens in a social order that gives us a fairly good return for the services we render it. We have adjusted ourselves—and pretty comfortably—to life as we know it. . . . Well . . .

"I will ask a question and answer for myself first. Am I at ease about the validity of my mental processes? As I was when I was rising twenty? No. Since then we have had our minds washed out by a real drench of psycho-analysis. We are beginning to realize the complex system of self-deception in which we live, our willful blindness to humiliating and restraining things, our conscious acceptance of flattering and exalting things, our tortuous subconscious or half-conscious evasions and conformities to social pressures and menaces. We take everything ready-made that we can possibly find ready-made, and there are a thousand moral issues, public issues, customary imperatives, about which—it isn't so much that we conceal our thoughts and are hypocritical, as that we *will not* think about them at all. We *will not* have thoughts to conceal. We are shifty even with ourselves. Am I overstating our subservience to the world about us?"

"I don't think so," said Dr Holdman Stedding. "No."

Davis said nothing.

"We have been born and brought up in a social order that is now obviously a failure in quite primary respects. Our social order is bankrupt. It is not delivering the goods. It is defaulting and breaking up. War, pervading and increasing brutality, lack of any real liberty, economic mismanagement, frightful insufficiency in the midst of possible super-abundance—am I overstating the indictment?"

"No," said Dr Holdman Stedding, with a sigh. "No."

"Quite a lot of highly intelligent people seem to be persuaded that we are heading for a world-wide war-smash—a smash-up of civilization they call it, and all that. You have denounced all that as blank pessimism, Mr Davis."

"Never mind what I have written," said Davis. "Sufficient for the present discussion—is the present discussion."

"Well, then, I may say the outlook for our world is, to put it mildly, menacing and disappointing."

Dr Holdman Stedding put both his elbows on the table. "For any far-sighted people the outlook for humanity has always been menacing."

"And not particularly now? Air-warfare, germs in warfare, the entire aimlessness of the unemployed, dissolving social cohesion, the rapid disappearance of mental freedom?"

"Yes," said Dr Holdman Stedding. "Yes. Perhaps—particularly now. For the things we value it is an exceptionally bad outlook."

"A general effect of things going to pieces—of large lumps falling down. Subsidences. And what I find most terrifying of all—and that is where the grim outlook for these Martians of ours comes in—the increasing *ineffectiveness* of any fine, clear thinking in the world. I don't know if things have shown themselves to you in the same light, but what impresses me most about the present state of the world, is the entire dominance of the violent, common mind, the base mind. It brutal-izes. It brutalizes everything new and fine. Inventions. Our children. Either it expresses itself in stampeding mob action, revolutionary or reactionary—it is all the same in the long run—or else it embodies itself in some Hero—like this fellow Hitler—identifies itself with him and so achieves its vehement releases. Assertive patriotism, mass fear, and the impulse to persecute—particularly the impulse to persecute—seem to me to be more dreadfully in evidence today than ever before in human affairs. Dreadfully and hideously. That's a question in your line, Davis. A question of historical estimates. Anyhow it is glaringly in evidence.

"We three sit here—lucky ones—we've got a sort of foothold. We seem comparatively safe. We've fixed up things for ourselves appar-ently. We may not feel quite so secure as we might have felt in Harley Street twenty-five years ago, but still we fell pretty secure. We are part of the intellectual cream of the world. And how much, I ask you, is it our world? How far dare we go out of this room and speak our minds about the things that are happening in the world now? How far dare we go even into the back corners of our own minds—with a bright light, with ruthless questions? Even you and I, Holdman Stedding, have been extremely discreet—and we are going on being extremely discreet—about this Martian business. We have our reputations to consider. We mustn't be extravagant. And so on. We are discreet even with ourselves. Do we let out what we really think about politics now, about all this bawling patriotism, about all this clammy, stale, canting religiosity, about such institutions as the monarchy? Although we live here in a free country! A free country! So we are told. No concentration camps here, no inquisition, no exile, no martyrs. No visible means of restraint—and yet we are restrained. How far is our intellectual free-dom here still ours, only because, as a matter of fact, we are too discreet to exercise it? Have we intellectuals here or anywhere any influence, any voice to arrest, divert or guide this stampeding of crowds which we call the course of history—?"

"Eh?" said Davis.

"These stampedes of crowds which we call the course of history."

"Go on," said Davis.

"Suppose we went out, to as public a position as possible, and said plainly what we think of human affairs today?"

"I suppose," said Dr Holdman Stedding, "they'd begin by smashing our windows."

He reflected. "The B.B.C. would probably let a leash of babbling bishops loose at you. And then your students would make trouble. Your back-bench students. . . . I'm rather in a different position. My professional gifts give me a kind of Rasputin hold on one or two exalted families."[58]

4

"I have been thinking lately," began Davis, and halted. He had the phraseological unreadiness of the habitual writer.

"You spoke just now of *stale* religion," he went on. "Such a lot of things in life now are stale. Out of date. . . . I agree. . . ."

He felt his way forward with his argument. "I suppose—I suppose all the main working ideas that have held people together in communities have been getting out of date pretty rapidly in the last hundred years. Strange new influences have been at work—as we three at least are beginning to understand. But because human society is a going concern, the main working ideas have never been replaced. There never came a definite time to replace them. They have been used in new senses, made ambiguous, expanded, attenuated. Replacement was something too heroic altogether. But each time there was a patch-up there had to be fresh strains and fresh distortions. Old things got used for new purposes and they did not stand the wear. So that—what shall I call it?—the social ideology—the social ideology has become a terrific accumulation of old clutter which now, simply through the wear and tear of terms misused, has come to mean anything or nothing. And to work less and less surely and safely. . . . Do I make myself plain, Keppel?"

"You put what I think better than I could myself."

"I'm in entire agreement," said the doctor. "Go on."

Mr Davis pushed back his plate and folded his arms on the table, after the manner of Keppel. He spoke with care. He held on carefully to his argument and both men watched him.

"And you see, there is a vast number of reasonable practical people who, the more they realize the unsoundness, and rottenness, to put it brutally, of their ideological framework, the more they are, as one says, disillusioned, the more they are terrified at what may happen if this vast complex collapses. . . .

"I have been," he added after a momentary pause.

"Practically," he amplified, "my life work so far has been bolstering up what I thought were still sound working ideas. I begin to see clearly through my own motives—for the first time. . . ."

Keppel sat back and put his hands in his pockets. It was plain he liked what Davis had said. "Here we are," he said, "in the palace of truth. And we find ourselves in virtual agreement that this world is as it were floating on a raft of rotting ideas, no longer firmly bound together, an accumulation of once sustaining institutions, customs, moral codes, loyalties, sapping one another, all so badly decayed and eaten away, that in the aggregate they no longer amount to anything much better than a vast accumulation of driftwood—floating debris.

"We all seem to be agreed on that. And now these new creatures from outside, these creatures we call Martians, are coming aboard our drifting system. With their hard, clear minds and their penetrating, unrelenting questions stinging our darkness as the stars sting the sky. Are they going to salvage us? Shall we let them even if they can? And if not what is going to happen to them and this mental raft of a world?"

5

"Mental raft of a world," said Dr Holdman Stedding, trying over the doubtful phrase. "Mental raft of a world!"

Keppel looked at his friend with an expression in his twisted dissimilar eyes, half defensive and half affectionate. "Well, isn't it?" he said.

"What's wrong with it?" said the doctor. "Don't answer me: 'Everything.' Be specific. What's wrong with the raft? What's your case, Keppel? I'd like to have it clearer."

"Well," said Keppel, and gathered his forces.

"It's a half-born mind as yet. Yes—yours, mine, and everybody's. Half born like a very young foal, encumbered by the foetal membranes it can't shake off yet. It is blundering about, half blinded and squinting. All our philosophies, the best, are no better than that. Especially—"

"Especially?"

"There is this secondary world which has worked its way into language everywhere, a sort of fold in the membrane that has established itself in a thousand metaphors, got itself most unwarrantably taken for granted by nearly everybody. Other-worldliness, the idea of a ghost world, a spirit world, side by side with actuality. It overlaps and lies beside reality, like it and yet different; a parody of it done in phantoms; a sort of fuddled overlap; a universe of imaginary emanations, the consequence of congenital squint. Beside every man we see his spirit—which is not really there—beside the universe we imagine a Great Spirit. Whenever the mental going is a bit hard, whenever our intellectual eyes feel the glare of truth, we lose focus and slither off into Ghostland. Ghostland is half-way to dreamland, where all rational checks are lost. In Ghostland, that world of the spirit, you can find unlimited justifications for your impulses; unlimited evasions from rational obligation. That's my main charge against the human mind; this persistent confusing dualism. The last achievement of the human mind is to see life simply and see it whole."

("That boy at Gorpels," reflected Davis.)

"But we're getting it straighter now," said the doctor.

"We've got new influences coming in," said Davis.

"But that isn't all," said Keppel, ignoring those new influences. "There's other things wrong with the silly creature."

"*Homo sapiens*," whispered the doctor.

"*Homo superbus*,[59] I suggest."

"Let's have the full indictment."

"The creature hardly ever becomes adult. Hardly any of us grow up fully. Particularly do we dread and shirk complete personal responsibility—which is what being adult means. Man is the boy who won't grow up, but he grows monstrous clumsy and heavy at times all the same, a Goering monster, a Mussolini[60]—the bouncing boys of Europe. Most of us to the very end of our lives are obsessed by infantile cravings for protection and direction, and out of these cravings come all these impulses towards slavish subjection to Gods, Kings, leaders, heroes, bosses, mystical personifications like the People, My Country Right or Wrong, the Church, the Party, the Masses, the Proletariat. Our imaginations hang on to some such Big Brother idea almost to the end. We will accept almost any self-abasement rather than step out of the crowd and be full-grown individuals. And like all cubs and puppies and larval things we are full of fear. What is the Sense of Sin but the instinctive fear of an immature animal? Oh, we are doing wrong! We are going to be punished for it! We are full of fears, fears of primal curses and mystical sin, masochistic impulses to sacrifice and propitiate and kneel and crawl. It paralyses our happiest impulses. It fills our world with mean, cruel and crazy acts.

"And what isn't purely infantile in us, is at best early adolescent. Our excess of egotism! We all have it. It is a commonplace to say man is as over-sexed as a cageful of monkeys, but sex is only one manifestation of his stupendous egotism. In every respect he is insanely self-centred—beyond any biological need. No animal, not even a dog, has the acute self-consciousness, the incessant, sore, personal jealousy of a human being. Fear is linked to this—there is no clear boundary here—and so is the hoarding instinct. The love of property for its own sake, comes straight out of fear. This terrified, immature thing wants to be safe, invincibly safe, and so, by the most natural transition, fear develops into the craving for possessions and the craving for power. From the escape defensive to the aggressive defensive is a step. He not only fears other beings, he hates them, he flies at them. He fights needlessly. He is cruel. He loves to conquer. He loves to persecute. . . . Man! What was it Swift said? *That such a creature should deal in pride!*"[61]

"*Homo superbus*, eh?" said the doctor. "But listen, Keppel. Is he really so bad as all this? Just a scared, self-defensive, immature beast squinting at the world because he has never yet learned to look straight? And hopeless at that? You experimental psychologists have been cleaning up our ideas about the human mind very fast in the past thirty or forty years. Very fast. You have been making this damaging—well, this salutary—analysis of our motives and errors—our queer little ways. Yes. . . . You couldn't have said a word of this forty years ago. . . . In my profession we say a sound diagnosis is half-way to a cure. Indicting the human mind is like sending a patient to bed for treatment. Maybe the treatment begins at that."

"Well?" said Keppel.

"Isn't the time almost ripe for a new education that would clear the stuff from the creature's eyes, stiffen his backbone, teach him to think straight and grow up? Make a man of him at last?

Davis shook his head. He spoke rather to himself than to the others. "Man is what we've got. Humanity is humanity. Starry souls are born not made."

6

"In guessing about these coming people," said Keppel, "there is one thing we have to keep in mind. A hard, clear mind does not mean what we call a hard individual. What we call a hard man is a stupid man, who specializes in inflexibility to escape perplexity. But a hard, clear mind is a clear crystalline mind; it turns about like a lens, revealing and scrutinizing one aspect after another, one possibility after another, and this and that necessary correlation. But anyhow, let us do our best to imagine how this—this infiltration of intelligence is going to work. No mighty revolutionary conspiracy—no.[62] They will begin to say things, question things, point things out. How will people respond?"

"Dislike certainly," said the doctor.

"At first, I think, they will encounter what one might call, hostile neglect. They will be said to be indecisive and ineffective. They will, you see, be up against the Common Fool, the Natural Man in either of his chief forms, either dispersed in mob form as the Masses, or concentrated as a Boss.[63] But the new kind of man will be neither, as the phrase goes, leftish nor rightish. Then, to be colloquial, where the hell *are* they? They won't be available for either side in the storm of silly wars and civil wars, the new Thirty Years' War,[64] massacres, revenges, and so on, Pro-Red, Anti-Red, into which we are plainly drifting. They won't count.

"That should give them a spell for getting together," said Dr Holdman Stedding.

"Not perhaps for very long. People will realize that these neutral things they say, these impartial suggestions they make, have a certain intrinsic power. They will be producing not fighting ideas but working ideas. Next, especially when the Boss side of the Common Man is in the ascendant, will come an attempt to annex their prestige and abilities in the interests of partisan governments. They will be asked to label their ideas *for* the Boss or *against*. If they refuse to be annexed, and they *will* refuse to be annexed, they will be said to be purely destructive, contented with nothing; accused of critical treachery. There are bad times ahead for uncompliant sane men. They will be hated by the right and by the left with an equal intensity."

"Then how," asked Dr Holdman Stedding, "will they ever gain any sort of control of the world?"

"How will sanity ever gain any sort of control of the world?"

"Yes. If you think that is an identical question."

"I am not a prophet," said Keppel. "I am discussing probabilities. But given this constant seeping of clearer intelligences into our world, may not this sort of thing happen? May not all these clearer intelligences, confronted with the same world, confronted with the same problems; may they not, without any sort of political or religious organization, arrive at practically identical judgments about them—put similar values on the same things? Without much confabulation among themselves. I cling to the belief that for the human brain, properly working, there is one wisdom and not many.[65] And if it is true, as Davis thinks, that one characteristic of this new type of mind is its resistance to crowd suggestions, crowd loyalties, instinctive mass prejudices and mere phrases, then without any political organization or party or movement or anything of the sort, may not these strongminded individualists everywhere, begin doing sensible things and refusing to do cruel, monstrous and foolish things—*on their own?*

"We assume they are going to be very capable, self-reliant people, able to do all sorts of things. Quite a large proportion of the scientific, medical, mechanical, administrative positions in the world are likely therefore to fall into their hands as they spread and increase, and their ways of thinking and acting are likely to infect all sorts of subordinates, workers and so on, associated with them. Yes. You have suggested already, doctor, that one might possibly Martianize even ordinary people by a saner education. . . .

"Well, then suppose presently you find an aviator in a bomber to whom it occurs to ask: 'Why in the name of blood and brains am I doing this cruel and idiotic task? Why don't I go off home again and drop this on those solemn homicides at G.H.Q.?'[66] And then without further hesitation suiting the action to the thought. And when he comes down, suppose one or two men on the ground agree with him and are not in the least indignant? And in fact stand by him. Even the Roman gladiators had the wit to revolt. The Christian name of the new fighting experts we are training for the air[67] in such quantities may prove to be Spartacus.[68]

"Suppose again you have a skilled worker doing some very delicate work upon a big gun and it comes quite clearly into his head that it will be better for the world if that gun does not shoot. Will it shoot? Or it is a chemist manufacturing explosives. That sort of thing will certainly become quite a problem as the Martians multiply. Your blustering demagogue or your blustering dictator feels ill and needs an operation, and there is either a disastrous patriotic quack who will make a mess of him anyhow, or some quiet, self-reliant but incalculable man with knowledge and a needle or scalpel, able to kill or cure. Why should he cure?

"The dictator will glare his cheap overpowering personality at him as far as his illness permits. Much a Martian will care. He for his part will be entirely un-melodramatic. It is your world against mine, he will say, and he will do what he thinks best for the world, and keep his own counsel. Power would be with the experts already, if only they had enough lucidity to take it. And it needs such a small step forward in lucidity."[69]

"But this is—sabotage!" said Dr Holdman Stedding.

"The only reasonable reply to unreasonable compulsion is sabotage."

"And you hint at assassination."

"I don't hint. Hint indeed! I speak plainly of assassination—if shooting mad dogs or rogue elephants is assassination. Assassination is the legitimate assertion of personal dignity in the face of a dictatorship. It is not merely a right; it is a duty. A sacred duty. A dictator is an outlaw. He has outlawed himself. He exists and he degrades you by his mere existence. He imposes filthy tasks upon you. He can conscript you. He confronts you with a choice of evils. It is surely better to kill your dictator than let him make you kill other people—directly or indirectly. You can tell him: 'You be damned' if you are strong enough; if that stops him you can be merciful to him; but if you are not strong enough you must kill. What else can you do? As a law-abiding man?"

"Awful," said the doctor.

"Plain common sense."

"No end of your Martians will get shot—if this is to be their line."

"They will be shot to good purpose," said Davis.

"Shooting them will do the old order no good," said Keppel. "There will always be more of these cool-brained gentlemen now. Trust those cosmic rays now they have begun. Trust the undying intelligence behind our minds. In a fools' world sane men will have a bad time anyhow; but they can help wind up the world of fools even if they cannot hope to see it out. One sane man will follow another; one sane man will understand another, more and more clearly. A sort of etiquette of the sane will come into operation. They will stand by each other. In spite of bad laws, in spite of foolish authority."

"A revolution—without even a revolutionary organization?"

"No revolution. Something better than a revolution. A revolution is just a social turnover. A revolution changes nothing essential. What is a revolution really? There is an increasing disequilibrium of classes or groups, the centre of gravity shifts, the clumsy raft turns over, and a different side of the old stuff comes uppermost. That is all there is in a revolution. What I am talking about is not a revolution; it is a new kind of behaviour; it is day-break."

"The Enlightenment," said Davis, trying a phrase.

"*Which is coming*," said Keppel with a sudden access of emphasis, "Martians or no Martians. . . ."

"But, my dear Keppel," said the doctor, "isn't this stuff you are talking just anarchism?"

"It would be anarchism, I suppose; it would mean 'back to chaos,' if it were not true that all sane minds released from individual motives and individual obsessions, move in the same direction towards practically the same conclusions. Human minds just as much as Martians'. Rational minds don't disagree so much as people pretend. They have to follow quite definite laws. We misunderstand. We don't pause to understand. We let life hustle us along. Every tyranny in the world lives— and such systems have always lived—in a perpetual struggle against plain knowledge and illuminating discussion. We are living—let us face the facts—in a lunatic asylum crowded with patients prevented from knowledge and afraid to go sane."

He paused and pushed the cigar-boxes towards his guests.

"A world gone sane," said Davis.

"Planetary psycho-therapeutics," said the doctor. "A sane world, my masters[70]—and then?"

CHAPTER 9

Professor Keppel is Inspired to Foretell the End of Humanity

1

"I wish, Keppel," said Dr Holdman Stedding, after a reflective pause, "I wish you would say something about the world these starry folk of yours—of ours—are likely to make here. In my way, as you know, I'm an amateur of Utopias and Future Worlds—and, God, how unpleasant they are! They come tumbling in to my collection now, a score or so every year. I sometimes wish I hadn't begun it. But if these star-men of yours do gradually spread a network of sanity about the world and stop what you call the Common Fool—Demos, *Homo pseudo-sapiens*—from ravening, grabbing, and destroying—just by barring his way, refusing to implement his silly impulses, and telling him plainly not to, then—can we, even in general terms, imagine the sort of world they are likely to make of it? What *would* a world of human beings that had, as Davis has put it, *gone sane*, be like?"

"Let us admit," said Keppel, "that this is attempting the most impossible of tasks. The hypothesis is that these coming supermen are stronger-witted, better-balanced and altogether wiser than we are. How can we begin to put our imaginations into their minds and figure out what they will think or do? If our intelligences were as tall as theirs, we should be making their world now."

"In general terms," persuaded Dr Holdman Stedding, gently obstetric as ever. "Try."

"Well, perhaps, *in general terms*, we may be able to say a few things at least about what their world will *not* be. You—what do you find in all these Utopias and Visions of the Future of yours? I suppose you get the same stuff over and over again, first of all caricatures of current novelties—skyscrapers five thousand feet high, aeroplanes at two thousand miles an hour, radio receivers on your wrist-watch; secondly, discursive minor novelties along the lines of current research; thirdly, attempts to be startling in artistic matters by putting it all in an insanely unusual and extravagant *décor*; and, finally, odd little fancies about sex relations and a scornfully critical attitude towards the present time. But these people of the future are invariably represented as being—I put it mildly—prigs and damned fools. World peace is assumed, but the atmosphere of security simply makes them seem rather aimless, fattish, and out of training. They are collectively up to nothing—or they are off in a storm of collective hysteria to conquer the moon or some remote nonsense of that sort. Imaginative starvation. They have apparently made no advances whatever in subtlety, delicacy, simplicity. Rather the reverse. They never say a witty thing; they never do a charming act. The general effect is of very pink, rather absurdly dressed celluloid dolls living on tabloids in a glass lavatory. That's about true, isn't it?"

"Lamentably so," smiled the doctor. "Nobody seems able to do much better. Some of 'em try to put it over portentously. Some make faces as they do it. But whether you preach about the Future or sneer about the Future, it remains, all the same, an empty sack that won't stand up."

"Alternatively to these progressive Utopias," said Keppel, carefully not looking at Davis, "the future world relapses into the romantic stench of a not very carefully preserved past? . . . you don't believe either story of course; none of us do; but the trouble is that we have no material in our minds out of which we can build a concrete vision of things to come. How can we see or feel the future until we have made the future and are actually there? All the same—"

"Yes?"

Dr Holdman Stedding was amused to see his friend descending into the pit in which so many a prophet had preceded him and perished.

2

"If we stick to general terms. *Some* things we may be sure of. At least—so far as my intelligence goes. This new starry race into which our own is passing is going to be clearer in every way—clearer—less moved, that is, by herd influences. Apart from their natural aptitudes they will have escaped all the mis-education and mental contagion that today nobody escapes completely. They will not only be abler people in themselves but they will be better educated. They will co-operate to make the world a world of peace. About that all sane minds must think alike. They will keep the peace. That Pax Mundi[71] will not be any sort of repressive peace. Why should it be? At a certain stage in the—in the *mental treatment* of our world, there may have to be a certain amount of fighting and killing, police hunts for would-be dictators and gangsters and so forth, but I doubt if intelligences more and more able to control the genes will need to eliminate undesirable types by force. Sanity will ride this planet with fine hands. No spurs. No sawing at the bit.

"Certainly there will be a World Pax. That is to say, except for the obstacles of Nature and the vagaries of climate, a man will be free to go anywhere he pleases and exercise the rights and duties of a citizen wherever he goes. An abundance system of economics and not a want system of pressures and exactions. Everywhere your needs will be satisfied. You will take no thought for the morrow so far as food, comfort and dignity go. No burden of toil in that saner world, and very little work that is not pleasant and interesting. All that is possible even today. To suppose the world saner is to suppose such things will be brought about. One is merely expanding the word 'sanity.'

"But when it comes to visualizing the new world the difficulties increase. To attempt that is in fact trying to anticipate all that will happen generation after generation in millions of brains, each one of them not only better than my own but better equipped. They will make a sort of garden of the planet. That seems reasonable. Probably they will leave some of it a wild garden. They will readjust the balance of life, which swings about nowadays with some very ugly variations. Who wants to see locusts swarming over cornfields, or weed-choked rivers flooding and rotting a forest district, or a plague of brown rats, or a lagoon crawling with crocodiles, or pastures smothered acre by acre, mile by mile, under blown sand? Making a garden of the world doesn't mean bandstands, fountains, marble terraces, promenades; it doesn't even mean the abolition of danger, but it does mean a firm control of old Nature in her filthier moods. And it does mean intelligence in economic life. No sane enterprise would give us ugly factories, hopeless industrial regions, intolerable noises, slag-heaps, overcrowding here and desolation there. Sanity is the antithesis of all that. It's the ape has made this mess with our machinery. Today we are still such fools that none of us can solve the complicated but surely quite finite riddle of private property and money. That beats us—just as the common cold beats us—or cancer. It tangles up on us and chokes economic life. It inflames our instinct of self-preservation to an incessant acquisitive warfare. A little matter of distributing our products and we are defeated.

"Serenity. Certitude means serenity. You may say what you like about this world to come, but rest assured that it will be not only a richer but a more beautiful world, as various as it is today and with all the beauty of land that is intelligently loved and cared for. Green slopes under trees. Glimpses of a proud and happy river. Mountains and the clear distances of great plains. I can see it all like that. Do you realize that in this world today there is hardly such as thing as an altogether healthy full-grown tree?

"And then about the way they will live, while still sticking to general terms, we *can* say something. We can be sure of certain things. The universe is rhythm. Throughout. There is a music of the atoms as well as a music of the spheres. Every living creature is an intricately rhythmic thing. It rejoices in rhythms corresponding to the complexity of its sensibilities. These masterful people with their control over materials, over all the forces of the world and over their own nervous reactions are not going to starve their aesthetic impulses. It is impossible that they should not have music and dancing in the normal course of their lives; that they should not have vigorous and beautiful bodies and that they should not be richly and variously clad. The variations will be subtle; you will have none of the clamorous grotesqueness of a fancy-dress ball. It is ridiculous even to try and picture that sort of thing now. Their music may not be our raucous bang, bang, bump stuff, their decorations may not be many repetitions of noughts and crosses, whirls and twiddles, but trust them nevertheless for music, architecture and decoration.

"And their social life? They are likely to be highly individualized, personally more varied, and so they are likely to find much more interest even than we do in assemblies, parties and personal encounters. People who don't find other people exciting will go into retirement and their sort will die out. Savages like gatherings; people like them just as much today; there are no intimations of any decline in social pleasure. I suppose these inheritors of our world will be what we call lovers, with a keen appreciation of the beauties both of character and body. I suppose that, being born of women and living interdependently in a large society, they will want and find satisfactions in companionship, friendship, partnership and caresses. Maybe they will pass through an emotional adolescence and have their storms of individual possessiveness, inflamed egotism, intense physical desire. The individual will repeat something of the romantic experiences of the race. That's still sound developmental theory; isn't it, doctor? Why anticipate a bleak rationalism in these things? Blood that does not circulate festers; imaginations that are not stirred decay. But these people will be going through these experiences in an atmosphere of understanding and freedom, with a better morale about them, a lovelier poetry to guide them, a pervasive, penetrating contempt for ugliness, vanity and mere mean competitiveness and self-assertion. How can we, who live in a whirl of sexual catch-as-catch-can—I score off you and you score off me—bounded on the north by what frightened people call "purity," on the south by the tout nu ballet,[72] on the east by a fear of offspring, and on the west by a sewer of envious ridicule, how can we imagine what the sexual life of sane men and women can be like?"

"Phew!" said the doctor.

"You disagree with that description?"

"I wish I could. But you draw with a heavy line, Keppel."

"Everybody wants to love," said Davis suddenly, "and everybody makes a mess of it. Every one. Suspicion. Misunderstanding. . . ."

It was one of those sayings that leave nothing to be said.

3

"You do give us," said the doctor, with the air of opening a new chapter, "some idea of these starry ladies and gentlemen, fine-living and full-living, who may inherit our earth. We don't see them directly, I admit, but when you talk, Keppel, it is as if we saw and heard the grace and colour of their brightly lit movements, dimly reflected on a distant wall. But they go about their business out of sight of us. Their business? Business today is mainly getting the better of each other and getting things away from each other. All that apparently is to end. No Wall Street, no Exchange, no City, no Turf, no Casino. What will their business be, Keppel? What will occupy them. What will they be doing? Can you say anything of that?"

"You make me feel like the sculptor's dog trying to explain his master's life to the musician's cat."

"But—in general terms."

"Yes. I think one can even say something about that. Every living organ has in it an urge to exercise, and the greatest pleasure of a living thing comes through a satisfactory use of its powers. Our successors will have incessant minds. Even we poor creatures of today use our minds and bodies in games and exercises and all sorts of rather feeble amateurisms, as much as we can. We hate being unemployed.

"But men who are keenly interested in scientific or creative work are very little addicted to games. Your games-player is a pervert who fiddles about with his mind because he is unable to use it, good and hard, for a definable natural end. Hunting was a great game in the past; and war, when you get down to it, is only a monstrously expensive and destructive hunting. For want of better imaginations. War will go when boredom goes. . . .

"But you need not worry to find jobs for the new-comers now. These heirs of ours will have their impulses to exercise skill, to discover and impose new patterns upon life, much more powerfully developed and much more intelligently adjusted. They will be enormously interested by research and by making and controlling things. They will—it seems to me to go without saying—be much more *alive to things*. Immensely— I really *mean* immensely—amused. Research and artistic exploration are full of surprises. They will be constantly coming on unexpected things. They will be busy, laughing people. Nobody can know the extent of the unknown, but the interest we find in life is only limited by our physical and mental limitations. . . . The saner the merrier."

Keppel paused and screwed up his face. "It is curious," he said, "that what I am saying now would arouse an intense antagonism in a great number of people if they could hear me. Here tonight we three are more or less in accord, because we have been traveling the same road together. Insensibly we have trained ourselves and each other. But bringing a human mind up against the living idea of progress is like bringing a badly trained dog into a house; its first impulse is to defile the furniture.

"Stupid people are offended by anything they do not understand or cannot master. They become spiteful and want to destroy it and banish it from their thoughts. I suppose if there were no guardians and watchers in our picture galleries, there is not a masterpiece that would not be defaced maliciously within a year. And probably defaced—filthily.

"But even contemporary man is emerging from that jealousy of what he cannot subdue. I am bound to believe our heirs will always find plenty to do and that this world community will be growing in knowledge, power, beauty, interest, steadily and delightfully. They will be capable of knowledge I cannot even dream about; they will gain powers over space, time, existence, such as we cannot conceive. Not even in general terms. There you are. In general terms—that is what I see before us. Like a great door beginning to open. Sanity coming, sanity growing, broadening power, quickening tempo, and such a great life ahead as will make the whole course of history up to the present day seem like a crazy, incredible nightmare before the dawn. That is what I believe in my bones."

4

"And that greater world," said the doctor, "really exists for you, Keppel? In such general terms as you use. But it exists?"

"Practically."

"Away ahead—not so hopelessly far perhaps?"

"Integral to this scheme of space and time."

"One might even, in certain moods, Keppel, feel a kind of nostalgia—?"

"One might," agreed Keppel compactly. And then: "My God! One does."

"And that music of theirs we shall never hear, that perfect health they will have we shall never enjoy, those enhanced senses—they are not for us; the whole world cared for lovingly, the very beasts subdued and trained by kindliness and every living man and woman with an intelligible purpose in life. That distant world. Have you *never* had a glimpse of that sane world of yours—in anything more than general terms? Nothing concrete with colour and substance, Keppel—not even in a dream?"

"Yes. I do dream. I dream that I dream about it. I confess it. Often. And when I awake it escapes me, it vanishes. . . . Dissolves into the turbid current of present things and is lost altogether."

For a moment Keppel spoke without restraint. "Lost altogether," he said. "Leaving not a wrack behind.[73] . . . Well, something *is* left. A sense of life frustrated. A sense of irreparable loss. Oh! The life that might be—the life that may be—the life that will be! This life that is not for us! This life we *might* have had, instead of these mere compromises and consolations which make up life today."

"Keppel," said the doctor, "let us be plain about this—you are fore-telling now the end of common humanity. No less. This would not be human life. This new world is something beyond all ordinary experi-ence, something alien."

"Yes," said Keppel.

And then he said something that startled Davis.

"That is where my hate goes," he said. "I hate common humanity. This oafish crowd which tramples the ground whence my cloud-capped pinnacles might rise. I am tired of humanity—beyond measure. Take it away. This gaping, stinking, bombing, shooting, throat-slitting, cringing brawl of gawky, under-nourished riff-raff. Clear the earth of them!"

"You do not even pity poor humanity?"

"I pity it in myself and everywhere. But I hate it none the less. I hate it. . . ."

5

Davis sat deep in thought.

"Keppel," he said abruptly. Do you *believe* all this—about these com-ing people? Or are you just talking? Tell me that clearly. Are you sure the world, after a few more troubled decades, a troubled age or so at most, will go sane?"

Keppel hung fire for a moment. Then he said: "No."

"H'm," said Davis, and then with a flash of intuition. "But do you *disbelieve* it?"

Keppel smiled the smile of a friendly and yet mischievous gnome. "No," he repeated with equal conviction.

"And that also," said Dr Holdman Stedding, after a moment's deliberation, "is my position."

CHAPTER 10

Mr Joseph Davis tears up a Manuscript

1

One day in October while that table talk of Keppel's was still very vivid in the mind of Mr Joseph Davis, G. B. Query, his Literary Agent, called to see him and discuss his prospects for the coming year. How was the great work getting on about which Davis had spoken a year ago? Was it sufficiently in shape to negotiate? What had he called it after all? The Glorious Succession? Sword and Cross? The Undying Past?[74] Our Mighty Heritage? Grand Parade of Humanity?

G. B. Q. couldn't remember. G. B. Q. had heard nothing about Davis for months. He was quite out of touch.

Davis stood defiantly in front of his study fire. "I've not looked at it for half a year," he said. "I've decided at last—I'm not going to finish it. Ever. It's on the wrong lines."

"But you had done a lot of work upon it. You even let me see some passages. They seemed to me quite a splendid beginning."

"It got more and more splendid. It became like an altar screen of saints and heroes. It became like a cathedral. It became like the great grotto at Han.[75] It became a sort of compendium of all the epics and sagas and all the patriotic history and all the romance and all the brave stuff human beings have told themselves about themselves since the very beginning of things. It took on more colour and more. It blew out like a magnificent bubble. And it burst. There's heaps of it in these drawers."

"But—" protested Mr Query. "*The Pageant of Mankind.*"

"The bankruptcy," said Davis compactly.

"You of all people! *You're* not joining the pessimists?"

"Have you never heard of the Martians?"

"But that I thought was just a pseudo-scientific mystification."

"It's a fact. Our world is in liquidation. We are played out. And they are coming, they are coming now, to succeed us and make a new world."

Mr Query considered this announcement. It was not his business to measure the mental balance of his clients. Davis was not joking. He believed what he was saying, simply and entirely.

"Maybe you will write something about that?" said Mr Query.

"I belong to the bankrupt system," said Davis, "one of the inconvertibles—one of the encumbrances. Gradually as our agreements fall in I mean all my books to go out of print."

Mr Query opened out his hand helplessly. On the spur of the moment he could summon no argument against this immense withdrawal.

"A new world is coming," said Davis, "and I have tied myself to the old. I know better now, but there it is."

Query roused himself to say something more, but he knew the case was hopeless even while he spoke. He didn't argue now. He lamented.

"Just now," he said. "When people need encouragement. They feel so doubtful. Where they are going? What is happening? Even about the Coronation?[76] Perplexing issues everywhere. Armament? After the Peace Ballot! America too. Profoundly unsettled. And now you too! Your book would have been a great success—a heartening success. A certainty. It would have sold like hot cakes. Even H. V. Morton[77] would have had to look to his laurels. . . ."

He stood up. He shrugged his shoulders helplessly.

"It is a very great pity."

2

Davis showed his visitor out and returned to his study. For a time he stood on his hearth-rug staring at nothing. Then with a certain deliberation he unlocked various drawers and took out a number of folders. He arranged these carefully on his writing-desk and contemplated the accumulation. He opened one or two and read passages. He grimaced, pushed his chair back a foot or so, turned aside from his work, and fell into a profound meditation.

The great book was dead.

It was stillborn—an abortion. He would never publish any of it.

"And I wrote that stuff," he reflected. "I *wrote* that. Only a few months ago. . . .

"I've done with it."

He repeated Query's words aloud. He mimicked his manner. "It would have sold like hot cakes. . . . A great success. A certainty. . . ."

He discovered a new streak in his own composition. What was it in him that had turned now against successfulness? he asked himself. What was it in him that was making him thrust himself contrariwise to his own reasonable disposition to go with the swim? What had divided him against himself? He realized quite vividly that people were eager beyond measure to be told that all was right with the world. Never had the market for reassurance, for brave optimism, been so promising than in these frightened years. It was true as Query had said that the piled MSS. before him represented a sure success. His phrase-making mind struck out; "I've done with lullabies. Let them wake up as I am doing. . . .

"Wake up to what?" he asked and started another train of thought.

Suddenly he felt very small and feeble and lonely, and it seemed to him that his universe, his immense bare modern universe, said to him: "*Well?*"

He felt that for a moment he must leave that challenge unanswered. A desire to go to his wife and talk to her arose in him.

He found her waiting to give him his tea. She smiled a silent welcome. "So you saw Query?" she said.

"I told him the great book was off."

"I thought you might do that."

"I haven't touched it for ages."

"I know."

He sat down on the sofa and found there a book she had put down on his entry. He picked up the slender volume. It was one of his earliest successes in the heroic style, *Alexander, or Youth the Conqueror.*

"You don't often read me, Mary," he said.

"I've been reading a lot of you lately."

"Why?"

"Because—I'm no good at talking, dear, and I want more and more to understand you."

"Latterly I've been trying to understand myself."

"I know that," she said, and poured out his tea.

He turned over the pages of the book. "I wonder what you make of this. . . .

"If you were really a properly cultivated woman, Mary, instead of being a wild, natural, poetic thing out of Lewis and Glasgow, you'd reel off a yard of trite criticism straight away. But you, being you, sit there, too wise to chatter. Because for you, you of all people, it would be an incredibly difficult thing to say, truly and gently, what you think of me. But that book puzzles you. Well, it puzzles me too now. . . .

"Mary, I want to talk to you. I'm frightfully troubled—in my mind."

"I've known that. I know. It is something about these Martians. I don't understand. But I feel it there."

"Tremendous things, Mary, are happening to the world—incredible things. It is time I said something. These so-called Martians—You have seen foolish and inexact things in the papers. You do not realize how close it comes to us, how nearly it touches us. It means something new in the world, a dreadful and terrifying newness. The world is being born again, Mary. And strangely. . . . I cannot tell you everything. But I have been drifting all my life, and all the time I have drifted, this tremendous thing I speak of has been happening to the world. The world has swung round with a sort of smooth swiftness into a new course. How can I tell you? I was deaf and blind. . . . Now I see. . . ."

He felt his great explanation was impossible, for the present at any rate.

"I want to rest for a time. I want to think."

"I have known your work was worrying you," she said. "Dear, I've known that. I have felt you wanted a rest. . . . Whatever I can do to help you."

"Bear with me," he whispered and felt he could tell no more.

"I must rest, dear," he repeated. "I must think things over. I must get things clearer in my head. I must make new plans."

3

He walked to the door of his study and she followed him. He stared at the files of the abandoned *opus* and with her at his side went across the landing to the nursery.

He surveyed his sleeping son for a while and then let his eyes wander about the neat, bright room.

"That's a fine big rubbish basket," he said abruptly.

She thought that a queer thing for him to say.

"It's a good basket to bundle things into when they get too much in the way," she admitted. "I bought it yesterday."

"It's a great basket," he agreed and seemed to forget about it.

He returned to his study and sat down there among the piled manuscripts. Mary after a thoughtful moment went downstairs. When she came upstairs again she went to look at him in his study but she found he had gone back to the nursery. There she discovered him seated in the nurse's arm-chair with that fine big rubbish basket he had admired before his knees. On a chair at his side was a large pile of manuscript and this he was taking twenty or thirty sheets at a time and tearing, tearing into little fragments. He was facing the cot. It was is if he was tearing the paper at the sleeping child.

"What are you doing?" she asked.

"Tearing it up. Tearing it all up."

"*The Pageant of Mankind?*"

"Yes."

"But there was such good writing in it."

"No matter. Nothing to the writing that will come."

He pointed to his son. "He will do better," he said. "He will do better. I'm tearing up the past to make way for him. Him and *his* kind—in their turn."

"No one can tear up the past," she said.

"You can tear up every lie that has ever been told about it. And mostly we have lied about it. Mythology, fantasy, elaborated misconceptions. Some of the truth is coming out now. But it is only beginning to be told. Let the new race begin clean."

"The new race?" she questioned.

He went on tearing and thinking while he tore.

Should he tell her what he knew she was? Should he tell her what their child was? No. The creatures must find themselves out in their own time. They must realize in their own fashion the reason for their instinctive detachment from this old played-out world. Maybe she was on the verge of that awakening. But it must come by degrees.

He glanced up for a moment and then averted his eyes from her grave scrutiny. He took up another handful of sheets and began to tear them.

"Every generation," he quibbled, "is a new race. Every generation begins again."

"But *everyone*," she said, "is always beginning."

"No. It has taken me half a lifetime to free even myself—even to begin to free myself—from religious falsehoods and from historical lies and from tradition and a slavish carrying on with the patterns of past things. Even now am I sure that I am free?"

"But you have begun!"

"I doubt," he said, "whether I and my sort are made for fresh beginnings."

"But what else are you made for?" she asked. "You of all people! Look even at this that are doing and saying now!"

And then she did a wonderful thing for him. She could have done nothing better. She came across the room to him and bent down over him and brought her face very close to his. "If I could help you," she whispered.

"You see, dear," she said, in a low, hurried voice, with both hands on his shoulders, "I know you are terribly troubled in your mind—bothered with new ideas that crowd and crowd upon one another. I know you are worried—even about these Martians in the papers. I know that. I wish I understood better. I'm slow. I don't keep pace with you. If I could—! If only I could! I feel very often I don't get what you are driving at until it is too late. I make some flat reply. And then you are hurt. Darling, you are so easily hurt. That imagination of yours dances about like quicksilver. Sometimes I think—you seem hardly to belong to this world. . . ."

She had a freakish idea.

"*Is it that?*" she said.

She moved round to look him in the face. "Joe! Joe, dear! Tell me. . . ."

Would the jest offend him? No. She stood away from him and put out a finger at him. "Joe! You aren't by any chance a sort of fairy changeling? Not—not one of these Martians?"

He stopped tearing the scraps of paper in his hand. A sort of fairy changeling? Not one of these Martians? He stared at this new, this tremendous idea, for a time. "M *e* !" he said at last. "Y o u   *t h i n k*   *t h a t*   *o f   m e !* "

The miracle happened in an instant.

A great light seemed to irradiate and in a moment to tranquillize the troubled ocean of his disordered mind. The final phase of his mental pacification was very swift indeed. At a stroke everything became coherent and plain to him. Everything fell into place. He had, he realized, completed his great disclosure with this culminating discovery. His mind swung round full compass and clicked into place. He too was star born! He too was one of these invaders and strangers and innovators to our fantastic planet, who were crowding into life and making it over anew! Throwing the torn scraps into a basket and beginning again in the nursery. Fantastic how long it had taken him to realize this!

"*Of course!*" he whispered.

His mind had gone all round the world indeed, but only to discover himself and his home again in a new orientation. He stood up abruptly, stared at Mary as though he had that moment realized her existence, and then slowly and silently took her in his arms and put his cheek to hers.

"You were star begotten," he said, "and so was I."

She nodded agreement. If he wished it, so be it.

"Starry changelings both," he said presently. "And not afraid—even of the uttermost change."

"Why should one fear change?" she asked, trying hard to follow these flickering thoughts of his. "Why should one be afraid of change? All life is change. Why should we fear it?"

The child lay on its side in its cot in a dreamless sleep. It scarcely seemed to breathe. The expression of that flushed little face with its closed eyes was one of veiled determination. One small clenched fist peeped over the coverlet. Afraid of change? Afraid of the renascence to come?

Never, he thought, had anything in the world looked so calmly and steadfastly resolved to assert its right to think and act in its own way in its own time.

THE END

Notes to the Introduction

1. The other novels were *The Croquet Player* (1936), *The Camford Visitation* (1937), and *The Brothers* (1938). In this same short period Wells published three long novels, *Brynhild* (1937), *Apropos of Dolores* (1938), and *The Holy Terror* (1939).

2. The film, *Things to Come*, directed by William Cameron Menzies and produced by Alexander Korda, is available on videotape and DVD. Wells's first "treatment" of the film was published as H. G. Wells, *Things to Come, A Film Story Based on the Material contained in his History of the Future "The Shape of Things to Come"* (London: Cresset, 1935). A screenplay and the release script of the film can be found in Leon Stover, *The Prophetic Soul: A Reading of H. G. Wells' Things to Come* (Jefferson, N.C.: McFarland and Company, 1987), appendices I and II.

3. "Books of the Times," *New York Times*, Saturday, June 19, 1937. One sees this formulaic reading encouraged even so recently as 1975, when the Manor Books paperback edition of *Star Begotten* announces "Science Fiction Classic" on the front cover.

4. G. M. A. Grube, "A Wellsian Lecture," *Canadian Forum* 17 (September 1937), 214–15.

5. *H. G. Wells's Literary Criticism*, ed. Patrick Parrinder and Robert Philmus (Totowa, N.J.: Barnes and Noble, 1980), 244.

6. While in the 1930s Wells was receiving less attention and respect for his fictions, he nevertheless continued to be treated as a man with important insights into the world situation. He published essays regularly in the British and United States popular press explaining the world situation and urging progressive policies. Some of these essays were collected in books such as *World Brain* (1938), *Travels of a Republican Radical in Search of Hot Water* (1939), and *The Fate of Homo Sapiens* (1939).

7. V. S. Pritchett, "New Novels," *New Statesman and Nation*, June 19, 1937, 1007–8.

8. Virginia Woolf, *Collected Essays*, vol. 1 (London: Hogarth, 1980), 327.

9. This sentence neatly acknowledges that complex thought, thought unlike that which Wells here claims for himself, is perhaps capable of finding a

"way round." But it also signals that such thought is in danger of getting wrapped up in itself and having no effect.

10. H. G. Wells, *The Fate of Man* (New York: Longmans, Green and Co., 1939), 1–2. The work was published as *The Fate of Homo Sapiens* in the United Kingdom.

11. Wells's advocacy of "ideas" in novels goes back at least to his arguments with Henry James. In 1911, Wells had disavowed the art novel in favor of a more "journalistic" novel that would engage current issues and topics. "We are going to write, subject only to our limitations, about the whole of human life. We are going to deal with political questions and religious questions and social questions. . . . We are going to write about business and finance and politics and precedence and pretentiousness and decorum and indecorum, until a thousand pretences and ten thousand impostures shrivel in the cold, clear air of our elucidations." ("The Contemporary Novel," in Parrinder and Philmus, *H. G. Wells's Literary Criticism*, 204–5).

12. H. G. Wells, *Babes in the Darkling Wood* (New York: Alliance Book Corporation, 1940), x.

13. Ibid., xiv.

14. Ibid., xii.

15. H. G. Wells, *The Time Machine, An Invention*, ed. Nicholas Ruddick (Peterborough, Ontario: Broadview, 2001), 69.

16. Perhaps the most radical of these investigations is *The Holy Terror* (1939), a long novel about a dictator who is treated very unsympathetically and yet seems to be essential to the revolution that will save the world.

17. In addition to *Last and First Men* (1930), Stapledon published *Star Maker* (1935), which imagines the richness of intelligent possibilities in the cosmos, and *Odd John* (1935), a story of a superman. In this same period he also wrote *Waking World* (1934), an eccentric and spiritual anticipation of a better world. *Star Begotten* acknowledges Stapledon as a precursor: "You know that man Olaf Stapledon has already tried something of the sort in a book called *Last and First Men*" (79). Wells and Stapledon met after the publication of *Last and First Men*. See "The Letters of Olaf Stapledon and H. G. Wells, 1931–1942," ed. Robert Crossley, in *Science Fiction Dialogues*, ed. Gary Wolfe (Chicago: Academy Chicago, 1982), 27–57; Robert Crossley, *Olaf Stapledon: Speaking for the Future* (Syracuse: Syracuse Univer-

sity Press, 1994); and Robert Shelton, "The Mars-Begotten Men of Olaf Stapledon and H. G. Wells," *Science-Fiction Studies* 32 (1984): 1–14.

18. Given Stapledon's interest in imagining higher mental possibilities, one can understand that he would be drawn to Wells's novel about "Martianizing," and it is a sign of his attention to the novel and its issues that he published his review of it in the volume of the *London Mercury* in which the final installment of *Star Begotten* appeared.

19. Olaf Stapledon, review of *Star Begotten*, *London Mercury* 36, no. 213 (July 1937), 296.

20. J. B. S. Haldane, "Messianic Radiation," *Nature*, 140 (July 31, 1937), 171.

21. In a letter to Stapledon, Haldane privately objected to the superman novel, *Odd John*, on the grounds that it alleviated the need for social commitment. "As a (not too thorough-going) Marxist I believe that man progresses to a better state of society by developing the internal contradictions latent in the existing state, and *not* by the godlike activity of great men (the fascist theory)" (quoted in Crossley, *Olaf Stapledon*, 225).

22. H. G. Wells, Julian Huxley, and G. P. Wells, *The Science of Life*, 4 vols. (Garden City: Doubleday, Doran and Company, 1931), 2:577.

23. Ibid., 583, emphasis added.

24. Ibid., 596.

25. Ibid., 605.

26. Ibid., 642–43.

27. H. G. Wells, *Science and the World Mind* (London: New Europe Publishing Co., 1942), 6.

28. Ibid., 7.

29. It is important to be as clear as we can about these processes. There is a reading afloat these days that sees Wells as an enthusiastic and ruthless eugenicist. There are certainly ambiguities in his language, and he may at times, like a great many people in his generation, indulge in thoughts of selective breeding, but he always returns to education as the mode by which the "race" will save itself.

30. H. G. Wells, *World Brain* (Garden City: Doubleday, Doran and Co., 1938), vii.

31. Ibid., 104.

32. William J. Scheick observes a similar difference from the genre of the scientific romance: "In contrast to *The War of the Worlds*, this novel [i.e.,

Star Begotten] offers no real plot, no solution or real conclusion, not even the certainty that an invasion is truly underway" (*The Splintering Frame: The Later Fiction of H. G. Wells*, English Literary Studies 31 [Victoria: University of Victoria, 1984], 83).

33. Basil Williams in an unsigned review in the *Atheneum* of *The Plattner Story and Others* (1897), reprinted in *H. G. Wells: The Critical Heritage*, ed. Patrick Parrinder (London: Routledge and Kegan Paul, 1972), 57.

34. This mathematical nonsense is corrected in the U.S. edition. Wells may have wanted the incorrect statement of the percentage to alert us to the sloppiness of the whole discussion.

35. The line is confusing. I take "more probably than not" to mean that it is more probable that the rays come from somewhere other than Mars. Of course, what gets smuggled into the logic is the presumption that the rays come from a single place (if not from Mars), even though that has been said to be false earlier.

36. We are in a pseudo-Popperian situation in which everything is true until it has been disproven. Karl Popper would argue against induction and assert that what distinguishes "scientific thought" is not its imaginative hypotheses but its refusal to accept any hypothesis that does not present a way of proving itself false. By a process not unlike natural selection, scientific ideas must be tested, and ambiguous assertions of the sort we see in the above passages, far from opening up scientific possibilities, simply render the assertions unscientific. See *The Logic of Scientific Discovery* (1959; New York: Harper, 1965).

37. William Empson, *Milton's God* (London: Chatto and Windus, 1961), 46.

38. There are many fallacies lurking in this argument. Consider the benign intelligence of the grizzly bear.

39. H. G. Wells, "The Informative Content of Education," a speech given September 12, 1937. Published in *World Brain* [1938], 110–11.

40. Wells's hostility to what Davis represents does not come through in the *London Mercury's* serial summaries, which, quoting the first page of the novel, describe Davis only as "a man of letters, a sensitive, intelligent and cultivated man." See the note on the text. Robert Shelton treats Davis as one of Wells's own voices and finds the *Grand Parade of Humanity* "clearly a reference to Wells's own *Outline*" ("Mars-Begotten Men of Olaf Stapledon and H. G. Wells," 8).

41. Wells, *The Time Machine*, 155.

42. H. G. Wells, *Mind at the End of Its Tether* (London: William Heinemann, 1945), 17 (emphasis added).

43. Shelton ("The Mars-Begotten Men of Olaf Stapledon and H. G. Wells," 11) notes the line "*Homo Sapiens* is at the end of his tether" on page 120 of Stapledon's own *Odd John: A Story Between Jest and Earnest* (New York: E. P. Dutton, 1936).

44. See my discussion of Heinlein's story in my *Rationalizing Genius* (New Brunswick, N.J.: Rutgers University Press, 1989), 74–79.

45. See Mark R. Hillegas, *The Future as Nightmare: H. G. Wells and the Anti-Utopians* (New York: Oxford University Press, 1967).

46. Olaf Stapledon, *The Flames, A Fantasy* (London: Secker and Warburg, 1947). This important novella has been reprinted in *To the End of Time: The Best of Olaf Stapledon*, ed. Basil Davenport (New York: Funk and Wagnalls, 1953) and *An Olaf Stapledon Reader*, ed. Robert Crossley (Syracuse: Syracuse University Press, 1997).

47. The theme of being taken over (or, conversely, of being in someone else's body) recurs throughout Sheckley's early work. The great statement of the theme may be *Mindswap* (New York: Delacorte, 1966).

Notes to the Text

1. Wells had a long, often strained, relation with Winston Churchill. Churchill was a man of many talents and of remarkable political and literary achievement. In 1940, after the war had begun, he was named prime minister. In 1937 Wells seems to have felt in harmony with Churchill, probably over their common objection to the way the Chamberlain government was handling Hitler's demands and predations. For a version (from Wells's side) of the relationship a decade earlier, see "Winston," a column originally published November 10, 1923, in *A Year of Prophesying* (Macmillan: New York, 1925), 63–68.

2. *Green Pastures*: a popular play by Mark Connelly about the stories of Genesis as told by African Americans in the southern United States. It was produced as a film in 1935.

3. In the second half of the nineteenth century the Reverend J. G. Wood published a series of lavishly illustrated books on natural history, one of which was *Wood's Natural History: Comprising Mammal, Birds, Reptiles, and Fishes: Five Hundred Illustrations.*

4. In England the "public schools" are what in the United States are called "private schools."

5. Dogmatic materialism: the term used by the conservative faithful for Darwinian evolution.

6. Technical school, i.e., not a public school. Wells himself went to local schools and the Normal School of Science in South Kensington rather than a public school and Oxford or Cambridge.

7. Confirmation: a Christian rite that strengthens the believer for the practice of the faith.

8. Wells himself wrote a history of humankind, *The Outline of History* (1920). Unlike Davis's, Wells's history argued a Darwinian rather than divine theory of history.

9. Echoes the close of the first verse paragraph of John Milton's *Paradise Lost*:

    > That to the highth of this great Argument
    > I may assert Eternal Providence,
    > And justify the ways of God to men. (I.24–26)

10. I.e., Davis begins his history at chapter 11 of Genesis, thereby avoiding the complications caused by the difference between the Darwinian and Biblical versions of the creation of humanity.

11. Paul de Kruif, *Microbe Hunters* (1926): a popular history of scientific understanding of bacteria, from the early eighteenth century to the twentieth.

12. The Prado is the large museum in Madrid. It has a great collection of Spanish art, including Francisco Goya's early-nineteenth-century paintings of war and human suffering. The Antoine Wiertz paintings in Brussels depict terrifying visions of human violence and suffering.

13. Winwood Reade, *The Martyrdom of Man*: an ambitious book published in 1872 describing all of human history with special attention to the importance of Africa.

14. Wells had great hopes that the airplane would make national borders irrelevant and thereby bring order to international relations. See his heroic aviators in the film *Things to Come* (1935).

15. Cantuar is the archbishop of Canterbury and the head of the Anglican Church; Ebor is the archbishop of York; the pope is the bishop of Rome and head of the Catholic Church.

16. *Defensor Fidei*: Defender of the Faith, one of the titles of the English monarch.

17. The theme of the anxiety of fatherhood turns up again in chapter 3, section 1. Wells himself may have had some issues about becoming a father. Immediately after his first son was born he fled, much to his wife's distress, for three weeks on the continent. See Norman Mackenzie and Jeanne Mackenzie, *H. G. Wells, A Biography* (New York: Simon and Schuster, 1973), 156.

18. *Undine* (1811), a romance by Friedrich, baron de la Motte Fouqué, tells of a water sprite, Undine, who is adopted by humans and marries a knight who later abandons her. Her water-goblin brethren taunt the knight and she disappears into the Danube. At the end she returns, kisses him, and he dies.

19. This seems a fictional name for a famous conductor.

20. The Old Testament Joseph refuses to lie with Potiphar's wife (Genesis 39). In the New Testament, Joseph's wife, Mary, gives birth to a child who is not his.

21. Greats: At Oxford "the final examination for the degree of B.A.; *esp.* the examination for Honours Literae Humaniores" (OED).

22. Latin author of the early first century BC. His great poem, *de rerum natura* (*Concerning Nature*) expounded the Epicurean doctrine of atomic materialism.

23. Stinks: Public school slang for Natural Science, especially Chemistry.

24. Bounce: "To talk big, bluster; to swagger" (OED).

25. Ernest Rutherford (1871–1937) helped develop the theory of the radioactive transformation of atoms. He was awarded the Nobel Prize in Chemistry in 1908. William Henry Bragg (1862–1942) and his son, William Lawrence Bragg (1890–1971), were awarded the 1915 Nobel Prize in Physics for work on X-rays. Niels Bohr (1885–1962) was awarded the 1922 Nobel Prize in Physics for work on quantum theory and atomic structure.

26. Assemblyroom: A large chamber in which balls are given.

27. Identified as Laidlaw on page 95, in the first paragraph of chapter 7.

28. The orthodox rejection of the Lamarckian idea that the inheritance of acquired characteristics causes evolution. "The crises of Evolution when they occur, are not crises of variation but of selection and elimination; not strange births, but selective massacres" (H. G. Wells, Huxley, and G. P. Wells, *Science of Life*, 2:583). This text goes on to argue that, though you may not be able to disprove Lamarckism, "at present it is quite impossible to see how such a mode of inheritance could work." Biologists "do not find that it explains anything that variations due to mutation, whose occurrence is known and proven, cannot explain equally well" (2.592–93).

29. An allusion to the famous opening lines of *The War of the Worlds*: "No one would have believed in the last years of the nineteenth century that this world was being watched keenly and closely by intelligences greater than man's and yet as mortal as his own; that as men busied themselves about their various concerns they were scrutinised and studied, perhaps almost as narrowly as a man with a microscope might scrutinize the transient creatures that swarm and multiply in a drop of water. With infinite complacency men went to and fro over this globe about their little affairs, serene in their assurance of their empire over matter. It is possible that the infusoria under the microscope do the same." Hughes and Geduld

note a number of other instances of this trope in Wells. See *A Critical Edition of* The War of the Worlds, ed. David Y. Hughes and Harry M. Geduld (Bloomington: Indiana University Press, 1993), 195.

30. J. B. S. Haldane (1892–1965), a politically radical English biologist, important for his contributions to the application of mathematics to the theory of natural selection. He wrote a review of *Star Begotten* in *Nature* (see the introduction to this volume).

31. Olaf Stapledon's *Last and First Men: A Story of the Near and Far Future* (London: Methuen, 1930) had received considerable notice. It was on the basis of this book that Stapledon had first made Wells's acquaintance. In the June 1937 issue of the *London Mercury* Stapledon himself would review *Star Begotten*.

32. Ivan Petrovich Pavlov (1849–1936): father of behaviorism. He was awarded the Nobel Prize in 1904 for his work on conditioned reflexes.

33. There may be an edge of self-criticism in this description of the assumptions of "pseudo-scientific story-writers." Wells here anticipates C. S. Lewis, who in *Out of the Silent Planet* (1938) has his hero, Ransom, attribute to "H. G. Wells and others" the assumption that extraterrestrials must be horrible in every way (C. S. Lewis, *Out of the Silent Planet* [New York: Macmillan, 1965] 35).

34. The idea of the "superman" (the *Übermensch*) and the phrase "Beyond good and evil" are indebted to the philosophical writings of the German philosopher Friedrich Nietzsche. Wells's friend George Bernard Shaw had done much to popularize the idea: see his 1903 play *Man and Superman*. Olaf Stapledon had very recently promoted the line of thought with his 1935 novel *Odd John: A Story Between Jest and Earnest*.

35. *Punch*: a fashionable British satirical journal founded in 1841.

36. Keppel here anticipates the title of Wells's last book, *Mind at the End of Its Tether* (London: William Heinemann, 1945), in which Wells despairs of the future.

37. For the English philosopher Thomas Hobbes, in his book *Leviathan* (1651), the Leviathan (the whale) was the autocratic state that prevented the anarchy of the state of nature.

38. Agincourt was the scene of Henry V's celebrated victory in 1415 over the French, and Trafalgar was the scene of Lord Nelson's naval victory in 1805 over Napoléon's fleet. Davis's book is clearly a nationalistic celebration.

39. Perhaps an allusion to Stapledon's *Odd John*.

40. Echo of Milton's "Lycidas," in which fame is called "That last infirmity of Noble mind" (l. 71).

41. Davis's vision is indebted to the description of the Martians in *The War of the Worlds* (see Hughes and Geduld, *A Critical Edition*, 149).

42. Albrecht Dürer, the greatest artist of the northern Renaissance, produced a number of allegorical etchings with hidden symbolic meanings. The notebooks of Leonardo da Vinci, containing a wide range of suggestions and sketches for inventions and paintings, are generally considered one of the great sources for insight into the mind of a genius.

43. Recalls in some detail the mysterious lens by which Mr. Cave seems to view Mars in Wells's early story "The Crystal Egg" (1897).

44. This paragraph contains a pastiche of snippets from Roman history, some of which are not as pretty as Davis makes them sound. Horatius and two companions held off the whole Etruscan army while the bridge across the Tiber was destroyed. Julius Caesar's invasion of Britain is treated as the high point of his career and important simply for the fact that Roman history is thereby tangentially linked to British history. Octavius, following Caesar, replaced the Republic with the Empire. The Punic Wars, fought between Rome and Carthage in North Africa in the third and second centuries BC, ended with the destruction of Carthage. The Pax Romana (the Roman peace) came at the hidden cost of severe repression ("the omnipresent cross for rebels") and heavy tributary taxes. The last line succinctly expresses two of the common defenses of colonial rule: justly "subduing" "barbarians" who might threaten the empire and bringing peace, law, and order ("assuaging the bickerings") to primitive people who cannot rule themselves.

45. Popular Christian hymn filled with righteous missionary zeal.

46. I Corinthians 13 is the well-known passage on love that begins, "Though I speak with the tongues of men and of angels, and have not charity, I am become as sounding brass, or a tinkling cymbal," and ends, "And now abideth faith, hope, charity, these three; but the greatest of these is charity."

47. In his *Experiment in Autobiography* (New York: Macmillan, 1934, 521) Wells describes the brilliant talk of Bob Stevenson, cousin of Robert Louis Stevenson. Frederick York Powell (1850–1904) was an Oxford historian

known for his work on the Icelandic sagas and remembered as a particularly stimulating teacher.

48. Sir Leonard Woolley (1880–1960): an archeologist who reported his extensive excavations in the holy land; H[enry] V[ollam] Morton (1892–1979), a travel writer who wrote about the British Isles and about religious locales.

49. His name seems to allude to Abednego, one of the three men who, thanks to the Lord, survived being thrown in a burning furnace by Nebuchadnezzar (Daniel 3). The allusion seems ironic: as the paragraph explains, Lord Bendigo has none of the supreme confidence and trust of his biblical namesake.

50. Founded in 1895, the London School of Economics was closely associated with the Fabian Society, the Socialist group that had pioneered economic reporting and in which Wells had been active in the first decade of the century.

51. George Bernard Shaw (1856–1950): playwright and essayist, a prominent member of the Fabian Society, and a friend of Wells.

52. *Protocols of Zion* is a notorious document setting down a supposed Jewish conspiracy to take over the world. Despite having been repeatedly exposed as a fraud, the *Protocols of Zion* continues to be invoked by anti-Semites.

53. Cf. Proverbs 13:12: "Hope deferred maketh the heart sick."

54. Thunderclap's impatience makes him the opposite of God. Cf. the lines from Isaac Watts's hymn, "O God Our Help in Ages Past": "A thousand ages in thy sight / Are like an evening gone."

55. Guy: "To make an object of ridicule" (OED).

56. Keppel is here approaching one of Wells's longstanding ideas: that a self-selected elite, what Wells calls "the samurai" or "the open conspiracy," will recognize its obligation to society and will band together to take charge. They will not become an oligarchy; they will be enlightened civil servants.

57. Another longstanding Wellsian theme. In 1901 Wells began forecasting with his book, *Anticipations*, and in 1902 he gave a lecture, "The Discovery of the Future," in which he argued that rational forecasting was possible and necessary.

58. Just before the Russian revolution, Rasputin, a peasant healer, had a

sinister influence over the czarina because of his ability to control the czarevich's hemophilia.

59. If *homo sapiens* means something like "man the knower," *homo superbus* means "man the proud."

60. Hermann Goering (1893–1946), one of Hitler's most important men; in the first years of the Nazi regime he headed the Gestapo. Benito Mussolini (1883–1945), Italian fascist leader who came to power in 1922 and ended parliamentary government in 1928. He titled himself "Duce."

61. I have not been able to find this exact phrase in Swift, but surely Keppel here alludes to the times in *Gulliver's Travels* when the King of Brobdingnag or Gulliver's Houyhnhnm master or Gulliver himself denounce humankind for its degeneracy and even more for its pride in such a condition. Many years earlier Wells had given similar words to Chaffery: "And, as Swift has it—to think that such a thing should deal in pride!" See *Love and Mr. Lewisham* (New York: Frederick Stokes, 1899), 208 (chapter 23).

62. Another reference to Wells's idea of "the open conspiracy," a voluntary gathering of enlightened and well-meaning people to organize the world along rational lines.

63. The coded language here signifies communism ("mob form as the Masses") and fascism ("concentrated as a Boss").

64. Thirty Years War (1618–48): European war between the German Protestants and the Holy Roman Empire.

65. A basic Wellsian premise would assert that true rationality is not conflicted or ambiguous. The idea gets further development at the end of this chapter. Words such as "clear," "hard," and "sane" imply this belief. See Wells's own self-description, cited in the introduction.

66. G.H.Q.: general headquarters.

67. One sees again Wells's faith that the airplane, which has changed international relations, will become an agent of sanity.

68. Spartacus led a slave revolt against Rome in 72 BC.

69. Wells depicted just such a situation at the end of his novel *The Holy Terror* (1939). The assassination of a dictator by a doctor attracted comment in the reviews of *Star Begotten*. See V. S. Pritchett, "New Novels" *The New Statesman and Nation*, June 19, 1937, 1007; anonymous reviewer, "Return of the Martians," TLS (5 June 1937), 427.

70. A play on the title of a play by Thomas Middleton, *A Mad World, My Masters*

(1608). For all his contempt for the traditional literary education, Wells knew English literature very well. In his early novel *The Wheels of Chance*, the draper's assistant Mr. Hoopdriver comically wonders about the value of the adult education he has received, which, as he tells us, included a course called, "'Lizabethan Dramatists." Mr. Hoopdriver shyly opines that "it seemed a little high-flown you know" (*The Wheels of Chance* [1896; New York: Breakaway Books, 1997], 244–45).

71. Pax Mundi: World peace.

72. *Tout nu* ballet: totally naked dance.

73. Keppel, perhaps triggered by the word *dream*, quotes some of Prospero's famous lines in Shakespeare's *The Tempest*:

    And like the baseless fabric of this vision
    The cloud-capp'd tow'rs, the gorgeous palaces,
    The solemn temples, the great globe itself,
    Yea, all which it inherit, shall dissolve,
    And like this insubstantial pageant faded,
    Leave not a rack behind: we are such stuff
    As dreams are made on; and our little life
    Is rounded with a sleep. *The Tempest*, 4.1.151–58

    The passage is echoed again a few lines later in the words "cloud-capped pinnacles."

74. This title seems to allude to Wells's novel *The Undying Fire* (1919).

75. Great Grotto of Han: a tourist attraction in Belgium.

76. In 1936 Edward VIII abdicated the throne of Great Britain to marry Wallis Warfield Simpson, a twice-divorced American. Wells was opposed to the abdication. Edward was succeeded by his brother, George VI, who was crowned May 12, 1937, a month before *Star Begotten* was published.

77. Morton: popular British travel writer. See note 48.

John Huntington is professor of English at the University of Illinois at Chicago, where he specializes in science fiction, cultural studies, and Renaissance literature. He is the author of several books, notably the seminal *The Logic of Fantasy: H. G. Wells and Science Fiction* (Columbia University Press, 1982), as well as *Rationalizing Genius: Ideological Strategies in the Classic American Science Fiction Short Story* (Rutgers University Press, 1989) and *Ambition, Rank, and Poetry in 1590s England* (University of Illinois Press, 2001).